MEN OF FLESH AND BLOOD

SHANE CHRISTEN

Seanchaí
Publications
CANNON FALLS MN

Published by Seanchaí Publications in 2018
First edition; First printing

DreamsofWoodandSteel.com

ISBN 978-0-9967756-8-7

Thanks to my wife for tolerating my hobby, my little sister for kicking me to get this published, and my father for getting me interested in history.
And last but not least, my friend Ellen for reading it and saying it didn't suck enough to be worth publishing.

Table of Contents

Author's Note

I have to look hard to remember when my passion - no, obsession would be the correct term - began. I remember reading a book on the Gettysburg Address as a youth but I don't really remember being all that interested. At the time I think I was more intrigued with Star Wars and World War Two. I remember well admiring; actually I think it was more awe and hero worship of the Legion members who had served. They were men who dropped their lives for four years to go off to foreign lands far from home to battle an evil the likes fiction has a hard time inventing.

So where did my fascination with the Civil War begin? I don't think it was as a youth, since in college my fascination was still with World War Two and the Mongol Conquests of Asia. My father asked me to see if I could find some information on family members who had served. I was very little help.

I needed an American history class for my major and the chair of the department was offering a two credit winter course on the Civil War. Professor Lybarger was a man who gave simple but poignant lectures with only one or two text books and a lot of suggested readings. The text was the very readable *Battle Cry of Freedom* and the Ken Burns Video series. We were given several options for our final; one was to pick a very specific portion of the war and research it or to pick a mistake or error in either *Battle Cry of Freedom* or the Ken Burns Series. Others chose specific bits of the Ken Burns series and picked it apart. I chose the firearms of the era and learned a lot from William Edwards seminal work, Civil War Guns. That class and that book started a passion in me but it was a slow starting seed.

Years later while stationed in South Carolina I developed a taste for Maurices BBQ and through a strange happenstance found a young lady there working at the South Carolina Historical Society. She introduced me to some microfiche of period newspapers and letters. I enjoyed studying the words of men who had been there. Those letters were written by men not at all unlike me or those veterans of World War Two. They were my age with dreams and hopes like mine. It was a slow growing interest that turned into a passion. Now through books and Living History my passion has grown almost to an obsession. The more I learn the more I want to know about those men. Luckily my passion has grown to encompass my entire family.

I have gained an understanding of the day to day life; day to day trials and tribulations that still haunt the average soldier. All in all I have garnered an understanding of our history; a knowledge that the more things change the more they have stayed the same.

This book is an effort, through fiction, to bring you the reader a touch closer to the men and women who served this nation so well. It is a story LOOSELY based on the lives of real men and women. Johan is a mixture of several men who served in various Minnesota Regiments. In every chapter an incident reported in a letter or diary is detailed, admittedly with some considerable poetic license. I have done my best to give this book the feel of the authentic events that shaped our country. While this is purely a work of fiction the events within happened near to how I describe them.

Who were the men who fought in the ranks of blue and gray? It is a question not often asked perhaps because the answer is so very complex. They were men as complex as those of today. Contrary to popular belief they were not all city slickers in the north and country bumpkins in the south. Their professions and experiences were as varied as they were.

They were men from every occupation imaginable and many that we no longer know; men rich and poor. From an apprentice apothecary to a zookeeper, a Regiment could boast experts in almost any field. In fact, one Massachusetts infantry regiment recorded well over one hundred different professions within its ranks. Is it any wonder that men like these thought themselves prepared for any obstacle they might face?

Those soldiers proudly wearing blue were often first or second generation immigrants. Recent immigrants from Scandinavia and Germany were quite common but representatives from Ireland and England, Greece and Italy, Austria and Switzerland were also in plentiful supply. Most who came to America came to flee the oppression of European monarchies, for the promise of freedom of religion, prosperity and a new beginning. America was literally the New World.

Those men were not always terribly well behaved; there were criminals and scoundrels among them. Gambling, various games of chance, sports and the creative language that accompanies such endeavors would become an art form in many Union camps. However, the troublemakers were the exception rather than the norm. The overwhelming majorities were family men; most were good God fearing men of the various sects of Christianity.

On the whole they were not a disciplined lot, especially the western troops, unused to strict military discipline. They would have made most professional European soldiers apoplectic. In the beginning they made good fighters but poor soldiers. But by the end of the war they were as fine a soldier as any in the world. By the time of the Grand Review it was widely regarded by European powers that the Union Army was the most powerful in the world. It was certainly the best equipped of its time and perhaps one of the most determined in history.

In short, they were men more like us today than we realize. Their emotions and motivations were little different from those today. Men worried about where the next meal would come from, whether there would be shelter to sleep in and whether or not he would be paid his wages on time. His family and loved ones were present in his thoughts of home and hearth.

Nevertheless, something always present in his thoughts was the enemy, whether on the other side of a mountain or on the other side of his sights. The enemy was a man just like him, and he was all too aware of it. Campaigning Union men all too often got a close look at Confederate hospitals and vermin laden camps that were little better than their own. On picket duty, he would often converse with the enemy sometimes trading goods and news in the process. By the end of the war the Union soldier in blue had faced the Confederate soldier on the field of battle and beaten him; but more importantly, he had come to respect him. Respect for a defeated foe helped those men to heal the wounds of war and to make the United States great.

The Private Infantryman in the American Civil War was at the heart of every land engagement of the War. Ten companies of Infantry (twenty-four with the Regular Army) were the fighting element of an Infantry Regiment. The basis of a company was simple. A Captain with a First and Second Lieutenant to assist him commanded the Company, four Sergeants and eight Corporals were his direct conduit to eighty-two artisans; privates of the infantry. The Infantry Company was rarely if ever actually up to it's established strength of one hundred officers and men. Sickness, disease and desertion often reduced a company to a shadow of its established strength. At times, companies could barely muster a platoon and in the darkest times, a regiment barely mustered a company. For the most part Civil War regiments who had been in service three years barely mustered the numbers present in a modern Infantry company.

Disease, boredom, terrible weather and the terror of battle would all contribute to dishearten the average soldier. Nevertheless, he would persist. While desertion was a problem in the Civil War; it was never epidemic. The Union Infantryman that lived to muster out of the service had rightfully earned his bounty and the gratitude of his nation.

Initially individual Companies within the State Regiments were raised from pre-war militia units, fire departments and even a few college fraternities. Uniformity of dress and equipment was ad hoc at best, especially in the first year of the war. A regiment might have a company of snappy Zouves alongside a company wearing Revolutionary War tri corner hats while yet another company might be wearing only what their wives and mothers sent them off to war with. By the summer 1862 there were uniform standards of dress and equipment, at least within the Union Army. However, lack of uniformity would continue to be a problem whenever supply problems cropped up.

Among the State Volunteer Regiments the men initially elected Officers and Non-Commissioned Officers from within their own ranks. Quite a lot of political maneuvering went into a commission or a set of stripes. While a popular or charismatic man might acquire a commission, it did not determine competence. Consequently, many obscure officers from the Regular Army quickly found themselves with a brevet to the command of companies and regiments within the State Volunteer Regiments.

The average Union soldier of 1863 was carrying a lot of gear, but it was all necessary to his survival. Luckily for him it was one of the most practical and comfortable uniforms in the world. A tin, wool covered, canteen carried the soldier's water. A tarred or plain sailcloth haversack was filled with his rations and typically a tin plate and spoon. A tin cup often was stowed inside or slung from its strap. His most precious commodities such as a bible, thread and needle and other sundry items were in a blanket roll or knapsack along with a spare shirt, blanket and ideally a couple extra pair of socks. A bayonet hung on the left side of his belt while a cartridge box and cap pouch completed the necessary tools of war. A loose fitting dark blue four-button sack coat was generally worn over an uncomfortable issue shirt or a privately acquired but more comfortable civilian shirt. A pair of comfortable sky blue trousers were held up by suspenders and worn at the heels brogans shod his weary feet. A bummer or slouch hat provided some shade from the sun and elements. A deadly rifle musket finished out the gear of the finest army in the world.

The average Union Infantryman starting the war was armed with almost any kind of long arm imaginable. A myriad assortment of rifles and muskets of different caliber's continued to plague the Union Ordnance department throughout the war. However, by 1863 the weapon carried by the Private soldier was likely to be either the superb Springfield model 1861 or the excellent .577 Enfield Rifle Musket. Both were outstanding muzzle loading weapons, in fact they were the finest in the world. A few regiments weathered on with substandard weapons but by late 1863, this was the exception to the norm. Breach loading and repeating rifles made their combat debut in the Civil War with the outstanding M1859 Sharps and in the spring of 1863 with the state of the art Spencer Rifle and later the Henry rifle. The Federal government purchased some ten thousand Henry Repeating rifles but their contribution was comparatively small.

It was the rifle, which a soldier kept clean regardless of the situation; it was his rifle that kept him alive and won victories on the field of battle. After the hardest campaigning a soldier's weapon was all but guaranteed to be serviceable and ready for action. While his clothing and gear might be quite a bit the worse for wear, his rifle was clean and serviceable.

All of this, with the leadership available to him and the, often waning, support from home contributed to the victory won by the Union in 1865. The Union Infantryman with the support of the artillery and cavalry and occasionally the Navy won a hard fought and well-earned victory over a tenacious and worthy foe. It was a victory that they could be justly proud of for the rest of their lives.

This book was not written to glorify the generals or to show the juvenile idea that war is glorious. It was written in an effort to show that the men who fought were men. A fragment, if you will, of the time when this nation was torn apart by four years of bloody civil war.

$\mathfrak{T}$he clash of bayonet against sword and the sickly wet sound a blade makes when it pierces flesh ended with a body crumpling to the hard-packed earth of the parade ground. The victor was a man in the full marching kit and uniform of a *Sergent* of the French Foreign Legion; the loser was a Lieutenant new to the Legion and only just arrived at this desert post. The victor's name was Johan Steele; the name of the loser was unimportant except perhaps to grace the stone over his grave.

Johan looked at the corpse at his feet and then to his bloody bayonet and wondered why it had happened. He looked between the body of the Lieutenant and the men of his company. He had not wanted to kill the man. But it had been a matter of his life or that of the officer, and as Johan was not yet willing to die that had not been a choice. Every man in the company had witnessed the attack upon him; attacking him with a sword was the unprovoked action of mad man. Perhaps it was the heat. It would not have been the first time a man had gone mad from the heat.

The silence that filled the small fort was the total silence of death. The normal buzz of a garrison was missing; even the mules in their shaded stable were silent as they looked upon him. The wind spoke with a sigh and the flag snapped in the breeze. The sun bore down upon him, adding its wicked heat to the almost unbearable silence. It was as though God were judging him from on high and all waited with bated breath for a verdict.

A low moan that grew to a piercing scream of anguish and pain brought that verdict; shattering the silence as abruptly as a lightning strike. Hardened veterans who had stood bravely the fire of Kabyle warriors at Ischeriden, Russians at Sevastopol and a score of other brutal campaigns flinched at the piercing sound. The scream came from a thin, small-framed woman with piercing blue eyes and brilliant white hair cascading down around a stunningly beautiful face. Johan had known her when they were children together in Amsterdam; now she was Kyrie.

He looked at her in surprise as she descended the stone steps of the junior officer's quarters. A rapidly growing understanding spread through him; he had just killed the husband she had spoken of. The look of horror on her face and her striking blue eyes riveted him in place as though he were pinned to the ground by a Kabyle spear.

He could see himself reflected in her eyes; a dusty, sweat streaked man spare of build with light hair and gray eyes and a bearded face. A man who she knew and had called friend since childhood, a man who now held the weapon that had killed her love. That horrible scream ended as abruptly as it had begun. Tears streamed down her face, her mouth opening and closing in a soundless scream of pain and anguish that had come from the very depths of her soul.

He saw himself in her eyes and knew how she must have seen him. Johan, a man she had called friend, stood over her husband with the lifeblood of her beloved husband dripping from his bayonet; the man she had loved more than life itself lay slain by a childhood friend. He looked at the bayonet on the end of his rifle and saw that lifeblood dripping from the edge. Blood wasted into the sand of the parade ground just as Kyrie's tears. For the first time in his life he wished that he had fallen before a foe.

Johan turned to Remi, his *Sergent Chef*, his *Copain*; he would understand, perhaps make things right. "I had no choice; he would have killed me."

The muscular Belgian looked at him, brown eyes flaring under the brim of his kepi. Women had always seen him as the handsome one. Where Johan pursued, Remi conquered. When the man spoke it was the sound of gravel grating; men obeyed and women melted. "I know. It won't matter; they will not listen. He was an officer." The fact that Johan would have to face the rope was left unsaid.

Johan sagged as though from a blow to the body; everything he had done, everything he had accomplished and earned in his life was now worthless. He looked to Kyrie kneeling beside the body of her husband. He would have to leave the only place he had ever belonged or face the gallows. He felt tightness in his chest; he was dying right here on the parade ground of this tiny little garrison.

"Murderer! You murdered him!" Her words cut through him like a blade. Her shock and horror had quickly turned to hate. They had been friends as children; she had come here to his home among the Legion to be beside her husband. He had destroyed her life with the same thrust to the heart that had destroyed his.

He stood beside Kyrie and placed his hand upon her shoulder. "I am sorry."

She knocked away his hand, turned and slapped him. The sound of the blow echoed across the parade ground like a thunderclap. "You worthless, thieving bastard; you stole him from me!" Her voice was as sharp as a blade and filled with hate.

Johan retreated slightly, as much from her words as from the slap. He looked at those piercing blue eyes that had once been the eyes of his closest friend. He felt himself stiffen, a fire began in his breast. If he was a thief, then he had best act the part.

"Then I shall do as you expect." He knelt down and yanked loose the money belt from the corpse. He straightened and wrapped the belt around his waist. She stared at him with eyes so filled with hate that he recoiled.

"I hope you die a slow and horrible death!" Her voice was shrill and strained by her pain.

Johan closed his eyes and drew in a breath, smelling her sweat and the rose oil she combed through her hair. "I probably will."

He abruptly turned from Kyrie and looked upon his comrades and friends. He looked to Remi, his Copain. "Tell them I had no choice… Viva La Legion!" The assembled legionnaires started and then smiled; their echo to him reverberated off the walls; it was all they could give him.

He walked out the open gate into the blistering desert never looking back. He was a dead man to them now. But they knew him as one of their own.

Charleston

Charleston was a major port city. With a deep harbor well protected from Atlantic storms, it was a common port of call for ships from Europe and Africa. It was one of the oldest cities in the United States, and fabulously wealthy. Some would have called it the heart of the old south.

Some still do.

Wilamina Mae looked down at her memory book. The book Mrs. Jones had gifted her in Paris was still beautiful. The leather cover was worn, yet still quite supple. It was her most prized possession and she dared not take it with her. If found among her few bits of clothing, then whether it brought a beating or merely a whipping it would still demand answers that she did not quite know how to give. This small book was all she really had to show for her life. Her recipes, thoughts, dreams and all of her hopes were now mute; no longer hers. Mrs. Jones had promised that she would be freed in her will; the grand lady had given her word. And kept it, too. But Mrs. Jones' niece, in defiance of her aunt's will, had sold Mina to a slave broker; and she was to be sold again at auction in a few hours. And so the book must be destroyed.

Mina had loved the ma'am, adored her. The woman had taught her so much, given her a life that few if any other slaves were ever lucky enough to have. Now she was gone, and with her, any dream Mina had of the life of a free woman.

Mina felt the tears come as she set her memory book into the cook stove. The flames began to lick at the cover as the fire reached out to consume the little book. Her only prized possession...

Perhaps there would be more dreams of freedom. Maybe one day they would be realized... no. She should have known the dream was futile to begin with. It was just that Mrs. Jones had always said the Lord provided.

The book was gone; only ashes and charred scraps of cover remained. Mina tucked the image of the little book into her mind and vowed to always remember what it had contained.

She looked around the house where she had spent the better part of her life. Not three days since the mistress of the house was in the ground and already it looked barren. The harpsichord Mrs. Jones played so well and so often was gone, sold to a planter in Kingstree the same night she had died. The paintings from France and the fine china Mrs. Jones had bought in London were gone as well, sold to a woman from Eastover the day of the funeral. The lace trim that had hung from every surface that would hold it was boxed up and ready to be sold, and the beautiful dresses from the Continent were packed away. The cleanliness of a house that Mina had claimed as a young woman, the neatness she had put there, would be gone in a week as everything of value was sold off by the spoiled niece, a woman whose name Mina refused to even think of.

With that thought, she whose name would not even be thought of entered the room. "Ah, here you are, little Mina." She saw the tears in Mina's eyes. "There there, you shouldn't cry; Auntie Ezra was old and it was her time."

Mina desperately wanted to tell the witch that she would rather see her in the ground in the place of Mrs. Jones. Instead she uttered a "Yes, ma'am," as she wiped the tears away.

"Aunt Ezra spoiled you; giving you all sorts of liberties that I would never permit in my house. But you'll learn your place with whatever house acquires you. You needn't worry. I can't imagine you in the fields. You'll end up in the house, I'm sure. I think you would make a good lady's maid and you are an excellent cook.

"You'll be happier that way. Why, you wouldn't know what to do with yourself if you were free! You'd starve!" Mina watched the simpering little wretch and imagined her hands around the thin throat wringing the life out of her... or perhaps a touch of Yellow Jasmine in her tea.

"Would you like some tea Ma'am? I can heat some water in no time at all." Mina was surprised by her own words and the thought that drove them... and she knew exactly where that yellow jasmine was.

"No, no, no. There is no time for tea this morning. I have to deliver you to Mr. Brooks first thing. Come along."

This woman would never be anything more than Mrs. Jones spoiled little niece to Mina. A liar and a thief, she'd taken goods that were to be donated to Mrs. Jones' church, sold them, and had ignored Mrs. Jones' wish that Mina was to be freed.

Mina was pretty and she knew it; that she would bring a good price she did not doubt. She was also of child bearing age, so a buyer would see her as an investment. At least she had that; she would be no $50 slave. She felt her stomach knot as she imagined the worst. There was no hope for her future and she knew it.

The life of a Legion deserter wasn't worth much; but if it was to be worth anything at all, it would be worth the most in America. It was said a man could make a new life there. At the very least he might disappear.

Johan looked at the city of Charleston; the United States. It wasn't unlike Amsterdam, if perhaps a bit cleaner. It smelled much better than either Algiers or Tunis. The cobblestone streets, market and massive customs house declared it an established city. It was a nice enough city to look upon, full of energy with men busily working and commerce evident in every corner. Still, there was something here he did not like; though he could not quite yet put words to it.

He walked out of the shade offered by the cool stone of the customs house into the stifling heat and humidity. The breeze was constant yet it did not cool the place, instead it carried with it the smell of salt air and the noises of a busy seaport. The sea air rode on the breeze and permeated the place as it did any seaport; its scent and the feel of it filled the very air and soul of the city.

The place thrived, money was evident everywhere in the glass, stone and brick of a city used to the strong storms provided by the Atlantic. Grand buildings lined the streets with their windows staring down into the cobblestone streets that were filled with the constant buzz of commerce.

His English was less than perfect and he knew that could bring him trouble here. He probably should have tried for a ship bound for New Orleans. At least there the language would not have been such a handicap. As he walked, excited voices and shouts caught his ear. Curiosity roused, he turned toward it. Turning a corner he beheld a crowd gathered around a platform. It took him a few moments to understand what he was seeing.

The place smelled of flesh and sweat; stale wool and sweat soaked muslin made the air close and stagnant. Yet it was full of men, all waiting upon the outcome of a sale. He had seen slave markets before; most had been far worse places than this. But seeing this, here, irritated him. So much for the promise of a land of the free.

Johan took his pipe out of his pocket and loaded it with the fine tobacco of this place. He ran his thumb over the smooth silver lid that covered the bowl and closed his eyes, remembering the bitter cold of the Crimea. His friend Sarro had gifted this pipe to him as the Cholera took him.

He opened his eyes as he lit the pipe and looked at his reflection in a nearby window. He had heard a camp follower call him handsome once, but no others had agreed; his piercing gray eyes alone were what a woman was likely to remember.

He scratched his beard absently, caressing the bayonet scar under his beard, and tugged at his frock coat. Even after the months at sea he still wasn't used to clothes that weren't part of a uniform. A decade as a soldier had made well fitting civilian clothing foreign and uncomfortable to him.

He looked around, taking in the people and seeing how they lived. He purposefully placed his back against the shaded brick wall of a purveyors shop and surveyed the street outside the market. The people weren't really all that different than those he remembered from his youth, though there were far more black faces here. Those black faces worked and moved side by side with white men; common folk all, but there was a separation between them. He walked into the slave market intending to pass through and if a wallet or nice watch happened to fall into his pocket it was all the better for him.

The auctioneer, a plump and sweaty man with a ridiculously tall top hat was finishing with a large and powerful black man who looked to have the massive hands of a blacksmith. Johan didn't quite understand the interchange but it appeared that the man had just brought the auctioneer seventeen hundred dollars; a fortune. He continued to move through the crowd and felt a gold watch slip into his pocket. He did some quick figuring in his head and realized that the slave with a blacksmith's hands had brought more than half of what rode in his money belt. The man at the customs house had thought it would take him most of three hundred dollars to get where he wished to go, and at least a month of travel. He had heard that the west was the land of opportunity and it was selling for as little as ten cents an acre in places. He wasn't really certain how much land an acre was or even how much ten cents was but it sounded like a lot of land for a little money. He had a month to decide what to do and how to go about it.

Johan was snapped from his thoughts by the voice of a woman; she was speaking in French with a distinctive Parisian accent. "Yes, I am able to speak French in the formal manner." The voice had a pleasant harmonious sound to it. He turned to look at the woman standing on the platform. She was petite and slight of build with skin the color of cognac. Her pronounced angular cheekbones and dark eyes with sharp eyebrows suited her well; she was handsome but no classic beauty, and yet her pleasant face captured his eye.

She was dressed as he expected a lady's maid might be, with a simple blue dress and an indigo headscarf. A few strands of midnight black hair had escaped from the headscarf, and he felt a strange desire to tuck those errant strand back under the scarf. From where he stood her hands looked soft and unused to the kind of heavy physical labor of the man just sold.

In his eyes she was everything a woman of class should be. But it was her eyes that snared him, captured his attention; they were dark pools of black opal. He had seen dark eyes before and they had always interested him. These eyes though were different; they held a gentleness and a strength. He felt as though he could stare into those eyes and lose himself forever.

The auctioneer grinned broadly at the audience and reached down to pinch the woman's bottom. She started slightly and blushed. "This likely specimen will teach your children all they need to know about high society and she might just liven up the afternoon a bit when the wife is off to tea!" He winked at the audience but his rough humor garnered no laughter.

"What do we start with then? Three hundred? There we go! The first bid to the fine gentleman from Sumter." And the bidding for human flesh began.

Johan didn't even realize he had bid until he had raised the price to five hundred dollars. Before he had taken the money belt he had never seen that much money in one place and had certainly never held that much. How much cognac would that buy him?

"Once, twice and sold for seven hundred dollars to the gentleman in the blue frock. Pay the man at the table to collect your property and papers.

"Now, lot one thirty-eight! A skilled craftsman; a genuine silversmith just out of his apprenticeship..."

Johan stood there a moment, a little surprised. Had he really just... *bought* a human being? He walked to the alcove that held a table and chair. The chair was occupied by a slight man in thick spectacles; the butt of a massive horse pistol was evident beneath his coat. He looked like a clerk to Johan, but the pistol made him a clerk with a pistol.

A man was bringing the woman; up close she was every bit as pretty as she had appeared from a distance. He stared into her eyes a moment. The small official looking man sitting behind the table said something to him but Johan failed to understand.

"Pardon?" he asked in a bit of a daze, the idea that he now owned another human being weighing heavily upon his thoughts.

The man repeated his words and Johan listened carefully; he still didn't understand but he could guess. Johan counted out the coins onto the table and the man pushed a piece of paper across to him. Johan relit his pipe using the action to cover his ignorance.

"Sign here." Johan understood that. He reached down to take the pen in his hand and made his mark as Remi had taught him. He looked at that rough scratching for a moment; could a man's name, a signature, really mean so much?

It must, for that rough scratching meant that for the first time in his life he owned another person. He had held lives in his hand before; that was nothing new. The lives of men placed under his command, some who he had sent to their death. The lives of those he had killed; murdered even. But he had never owned someone and he was certain he didn't care for the feeling.

He looked to his purchase; she stood there holding a small valise. "You can read and write?" he demanded in French, his eyes drawn to that errant strand of hair.

Dark eyes went suddenly wary, but she replied with a Parisian accent. "Yes, sir."

"In English too? Johan asked.

The guarded look spread to her face, then disappeared into a neutral expression. "The Ma'am was mostly blind; she told me what to write, and I was also required to read her letters to her."

"You will have the same task then." Johan motioned for her to follow with a slight smile as he walked away from the slave market. "Your name, what is it?"

"Wilamina Mae." Her reply was quick, she was proud of her name.

"I am Johan, Johan Steele. Tell me about yourself."

She smiled like she was about to laugh, then looked uncomfortable. "I was born here, sir. When I was just a child I was bought and made the maid of a grand lady. She was wealthy and she traveled. She took me with her to England and then France... to Paris. When she went blind and I wrote letters for her and read her mail and books to her. She died and her niece sold me.

"I will be happy to perform the same services for your wife. I am also a good cook and housekeeper."

"I am not married; I am going west." Johan said quietly, half listening to his heels ring against the cobblestones.

"Oh." She stopped a moment, a look of apprehension crossing her face.

Johan grinned. "You will teach me the English, you will cook for me, mend my clothes and such. You will come west with me and then we shall see. Now come, my lodgings are just ahead between Church and State Streets I must make many purchases and you will be my English voice."

He considered a moment. "When I told you my name, you looked about to laugh. Why?"

Now she looked embarrassed. "Your name, sir. It sounds like one of the heroes from the novels I used to read my former lady."

Johan laughed. "Johan has been my name as long as I can remember, and I am no hero. I chose Steele when I joined..." the words failed as the memories surged in his mind. After a moment he finished, "...when I became a man."

She looked at him oddly but said nothing more.

Johan sat down on the bench and marveled; cushions, soft and comfortable. He liked it, this traveling by the rails. It was a damned sight better than marching at the tail end of a column choking on the dust kicked up by a thousand men before you, all the while praying for just a sip of brackish water to sate the thirst.

He watched Mina sit down on the bench across from him. That blue dress she wore complimented her eyes and skin; she noticed his look and blushed slightly.

For her he had purchased a set of traveling clothes, a simple but strong wooden trunk, and a box full of cooking gear. He had been careful to select only the most robust among the choices; the kind of equipage that would campaign well.

Then a couple sets of clothing and a wide brimmed hat for him, a half a dozen blankets, a good spade, ax and hatchet as well as a strong tent. He had also selected a rifle, an American-made copy of the excellent P1853 Enfield by a company called Windsor. It was far superior to any weapon he had ever carried and he very much liked the balance and feel of it. The rifling was good and the lock crisp; it had seen no real use. The bullet it fired was considerably smaller than what he was used to, but he expected it would do the job when needed.

The shopkeeper had tried to sell him a pistol as well but Johan had scoffed at the idea; pistols were for officers or dandies and he was neither. He *had* purchased a good strong knife with a straight double edged blade that would hold a razor edge. He had also bought a bottle of good cognac; the first real liquor he had seen in many months. It called to him so much that he could almost taste it through the bottle.

He looked at Mina again. Her French was the kind he would expect in Paris, or possibly from the monied class. His own French had been started in the streets of Amsterdam and finished in the Legion with a mouthful of rocks. But more than ten years speaking it had made him proficient.

She was such a pretty woman, far prettier than most that he had known. And there was no arrogance in her, though she was honest to a fault and quite smart. She did not flaunt that intelligence. In fact the reverse was true - she made real efforts to hide it. He understood that. He was ignorant in many things and didn't like the idea of having that ignorance thrown in his face.

Though it was not for his benefit that she hid her intelligence, he knew. Ignorance was expected of a black woman and she was wise enough to know to give those in power what they wanted... or the illusion of it. At times she seemed quite naïve, and he did not think it an act. He looked at her, studying her pleasant shape and gaze-capturing facial features.

He felt the car lurch and the train began to pull away from the station. Johan looked out the window. He knew where he was going generally. While crossing the Atlantic he had struck up a friendship with a Voyageur; a man who had made his fortune thirty years ago, trading furs with the Red Indian along a river called the Minnesota. Johan had listened to what the man had to say and learned much. Including that the Red Indians spoke French and preferred to deal with the French than either the English or Americans. The Minnesota. It had a good sound, he was going to make his future trading with the Red Indians.

He glanced again at Mina and shook his head slightly. He still had a hard time believing that he had bought her. It had been something of a whim, perhaps a foolish one. Her French had called to him... and there was also great use in her presence. He needed someone to translate for him and to teach him the American English, after all. He spoke some, enough to communicate, but he had learned what little he knew from a Scotsman in the Crimea. If he was to make a life here he would have to learn the language the way they spoke it. She was the avenue to that.

"You shouldn't look at me so. It isn't proper. I shouldn't even be in the same car with the white folk." Her voice was low and quiet; to a man used to barking commands on a parade ground it was nothing more than a pleasant whisper. Johan snorted with contempt at her words. Mina looked at him with those captivating brown eyes.

"You are a beautiful woman. Certainly far prettier than any others on this train. You are also my teacher. If there are complaints I will explain that to them." Johan allowed a smile to cross his face. It was a vicious look, the kind that frightened people, and well it should. Remi had told him once that his smile was a gift from the devil.

She shook her head. "Master, do you not understand? This is not France. A colored woman…"

"Do not call me master again," he interrupted harshly. "I am Johan or Monsieur Steele, but not master. When we reach the Minnesota I will let you go to be free. By then you will have taught me the English."

Her face brightened and her eyes widened in surprise. "Free…"

Mina looked across the passenger compartment at her new master smoking his pipe. This man who had paid so much for her was a far cry from Mrs. Jones. She had been a grand woman, gentle and kind; a truly good lady. Mina felt the grief well up inside of her at the thought of her lost mistress. That was a pain even deeper than the lost promise of freedom. And yet, now that she was the property of this

Monsieur Steele, the hope was to be rekindled? Would the hope stand good this time?

It would depend on the manner of man this Johan truly was.

So what was he? He had the money of a gentleman but not the manner; he was rough and cold, cold as the steel in his false surname. Would he want her in his bed?

The Ma'am had been a woman wise to the world, and the ways and means of men, passing much of that knowledge to her So Mina knew what to look for in men, how to judge them. But until now she had never been forced to really look at a man in that way.

He didn't look at her with the lust she had seen in the eyes of other men; in fact his eyes seemed dead. She imagined those eyes were like that of some kind of wild animal. This was a dangerous man. How she knew that was true she couldn't say, but there was no shadow of doubt in her mind.

His accent was not a familiar one. He hadn't learned his French in any wealthy Parisian school, that was certain. In fact she was sure French was not his native tongue. She supposed his accent might have been from one of the Low Countries though she had no idea which.

Mina wondered; did other women think him handsome? He rarely smiled, and when he did she was quite uncomfortable. An alligator smiled something like that, she fancied. His gray eyes seemed to see clean through whoever he looked at and when they settled on her... Cold eyes, the color of a good kitchen knife. As for his age, she might have guessed early to middle thirties, but she really had nothing to measure it against. What might he look like without his beard? Younger, probably. But the beard suited him; it fit his face and looked right upon him. He didn't look comfortable in his frock coat; he kept tugging at it like it failed to fit him properly even though it was obviously a quality garment.

Her gaze was drawn downward. The Ma'am had always said you could tell a lot by a man's shoes. It was a way to take a measure of a man. If they were filthy and unkempt the man would be as well. But if they were carefully cared for yet worn and clean it meant the man would likely be the same. Showy and uncomfortable or functional and comfortable were all things to compare between footwear and the man. It had made great sense at the time but now Mina wasn't quite so sure. His boots were clean and carefully taken care of, but they were far from new. She could see an uneven wear on the right heel from where she sat, heavy wear evident despite the metal heel plates and hobnails. It meant he likely walked on the edge of his feet; that had to be uncomfortable.

The Ma'am had also taught you could judge a person by what they purchased. If true, then this was a simple man. When he had taken her into the dry goods store he had purchased her a set of simple, practical traveling clothes and had then asked her what she needed to cook with. He had *asked* her, not told her, and then had listened. He hadn't bought everything she had suggested but he had bought some of it and a few things she hadn't thought of.

She hadn't really expected him to buy her anything, so the new clothes and boots were a surprise. The mirror and beautifully carved comb had been an outright shock. Did he know that the hatpin he had bought her was a very good weapon? Strong metal, it was with a sharp point. She considered a moment; he almost certainly did. Well, she would keep it under her pillow at night just the same.

Mina wasn't certain why he had bought so many blankets or so many of those good quality kitchen knives. The rifle he had selected was made by Windsor for the British Army. She didn't really understand what that meant, but she had watched the way Mr. Steele had handled it. His air had been that of a man long familiar with weapons and their use. Twenty-five dollars for a rifle seemed terribly expensive to her, but he had paid for it as though it was nothing. He had bargained for other items, but not that rifle. The shopkeeper had tried to sell him a fine Colt pistol as well but he had laughed and bought a vicious looking knife instead and again he hadn't tried to bargain.

The bottle of expensive cognac worried her. He had looked at it with real lust; was liquor his vice? The Ma'am had said all men had one, whether it be gambling, liquor, women or something else. Was cognac his?

Mina looked down at the basket full of yarn at her feet and picked up the two ebony needles he had bought her. She had always loved the feel of yarn as it twisted through her fingers, with the tiny knots slowly coming together to create something, whether it be socks or a scarf for the Ma'am. It was something she was good at and it had always passed the time. And of course she could cook. As the Ma'am had been unwilling to pay for a cook to prepare meals for just the two of them, it had fallen on Mina to prepare their meals. She had no doubt this man who called himself Johan Steele would appreciate her food as well.

She looked at him. What was he thinking, as the tobacco smoke curled lazily from the pipe. "Sir, we are traveling by train, I am knitting. In English that would be…"

Vicksburg

Vicksburg was a hub where roads met rail lines and the mighty Mississippi River. In the 1850's Vicksburg grew dramatically, becoming a major regional city. But with that rapid growth, the criminal element followed.

"Y̸ou are obviously a man of means, sir. My daughter and I would be honored if you were to call."

The woman who spoke was not large, but she was wide, shaped a little like an egg, and she carried herself with an arrogance that irritated Johan. She might have been attractive in her youth, but the years wore heavily upon her as did, apparently, a fondness for sweets. The daughter she spoke of was no woman, but a child at most twelve years of age.

The girl herself was fine featured and pretty, with hands soft from an easy upbringing. The young eyes were truly lovely; the color of the sea with tiny speckles of white gold that reminded him of the froth on the waves. That striking gaze looked up at him from under fluttering eyelids, and the long auburn hair that framed her face suited her.

She would likely grow to be a beauty, but for now she was merely a child. A spoiled child at that, obviously unused to the simplest work. That, more than anything, repulsed him.

Johan felt himself smile slightly. She was attempting to be both demure and seductive at once, and to a man who had watched women ply their bodies as a profession it was as amusing as it was amateurish. But he had spent his formative years working in a brothel, and so she and her mother were transparent. And revolting, in the case of the mother.

"Pardon madam; I shall be boarding upon the steamboat this afternoon and… How do you say in English? I have no… interest. Perhaps when I return from my travels we shall meet again." He was trying not to be curt, but this woman was irritating him.

Perhaps it was his knowledge that the vilest of pimps were women.

"No interest? What manner of gentleman has no interest in calling upon ladies of good social standing?"

Johan sighed to himself. And now nothing he said would placate her. She would work herself into a fit, causing a scene calculated to garner attention and embarrass him into submission.

Mina interrupted. "Madame, I think Monsieur Steele meant 'no time.' He has only recently learned English."

The woman paused. Johan watched her size up Mina, visibly calculating her value, and ground his teeth. "I see; I'm sure no offense was intended. As an apology I will accept the gentleman calling for tea."

"No,"Johan said firmly, "I meant no interest. I have the boat to meet, and I will not take later passage so that you might attempt to make a husband of me for your child. She is lovely, but is still a child. Find a good man and have him give you grandchildren; do not look to me. I have business to conduct and no time for a wife. Good day madam."

Johan turned on his heel and walked toward the river-front. Johan switched to the more familiar French. "Come Ms. Mina, I have need of your translations, and I cannot tolerate such a woman."

From the corner of his eye he could see Mina trying to hold back a smile. The mother and her child both looked horrified.

"You, sir, are no gentleman!" the mother exclaimed.

Johan turned and looked coldly at the woman. He felt that old grin spread across his face; the woman flinched as he stared into eyes not half so pretty as those of her daughter. "Madame, I have never said I was."

Mina watched the packing of her master's goods into a compact bundle; the men from the riverboat knew what they were about and worked efficiently and quickly. Their knots were secure and the way they worked identified them as men who knew their trade. She wondered how large the hold on this boat was; there were so many things. Though to be fair most of it was quite compact and with the exception of the pots and pans it was fairly light.

The masses of people here surprised her; the bustle of Vicksburg was not what she expected. There were hundreds of people in the street and better than fifty riverboats along the shore. People from all walks of life packed the streets, from hardscrabble farmers and their families with wagons full of supplies to wealthy plantation owners in gilded carriages with a score of slaves answering their every whim. Mina could see the poorest women wearing simple sack dresses and women wearing the latest Parisian fashions within feet of each other. This city was truly a crossroads with people of all walks of life coming together from all over the world.

The city was built on the side of a hill with all the emphasis of the city upon the riverfront with its scores of river craft. Parts of the city had made real attempts to look like Charleston or some other established city. There were many lovely homes and public buildings. The features of a city, but close by them stood ramshackle wooden huts that made the slave quarters of her childhood look like majestic palaces.

They had arrived yesterday after having changed trains twice on the way west. Johan was worried that his goods would not be properly transferred and had supervised each transfer. He was doing so again, making certain that his goods were safely and completely transferred. He knew his business; checking knots and the tightness of ropes holding bundles together. He knew exactly what was in each bundle and how large it needed to be for it to be complete.

Mina watched Johan inspect his goods. He was still so strange, with so many contradictions. While his clothing was that of a gentleman, his manner was not. Nothing about him was smooth and pampered, and there was no sophistication in his manner. His hands were powerful, and appeared as hard-used as his boots. Yet he had such funds as she could only dream of, and only gentlemen would have such wealth. Although... even in his monies he contradicted. The money was merely worn, it was not a part of him like so many rich folk that she had been around.

There was something about that attitude that she liked. He did not waste it - there was nothing spent on frills - but money still flowed through his fingers. He demanded his monies' worth for everything he purchased, of course, but was not unwilling to part with his funds when it was appropriate. He didn't gamble and he never looked twice at the houses of ill repute...

Ah, but he did drink. Always there was a pipe in his mouth or a glass of fine Cognac in his hand. She had little doubt that he would have been quite willing to forgo the glass altogether and drink straight from the bottle. He did not though. That in itself was a measure of the man.

Where and how had he acquired the money? She would never ask. Had he inherited his fortune? That might account for his seeming discomfort with coin. Or it might be the attention it garnered that made him uncomfortable. From the moment they had stepped off the train in Vicksburg Johan had been noticed; first by the pickpocket that tried to lift his gold watch, and then by the woman trying to marry away her daughter.

Both had been a sight to see. The pickpocket had been a boy not more than twelve. How Johan had detected the thief was a mystery to her, but his actions had been memorable to all who had watched. He had laughed, then grabbed the boy by the britches and hauled him back next to him.

The boy had been filthy; an urchin by any stretch of the imagination and yet Johan had not flinched in the slightest when confronted with such filth. He hadn't turned the child over to the law either, but had bought the boy a meal and had a long talk with him instead.

All in the saloon had looked askance at Johan as he dragged the boy in by his collar with Mina walking behind. But he had ignored the looks as he dropped the boy into a chair next to an empty table.

"Meat and potatoes for the boy and I will have a bottle of your best cognac." Johan had sounded amused as he gave his order to the scowling barkeep.

"We don't serve niggers here, mister." The barkeep was a big man with massive shoulders and a face was marked with the scars of the pox. His eyes were almost yellow and full of malevolence. If Mina could imagine a face of evil, this would have been it.

Johan looked to the boy. "Nigger? The boy just needs a bath."

"I mean the woman," the barkeep growled.

Johan laughed harshly. "She is an Indian woman, a breed. Do I look like I could afford a slave to follow my every whim?"

The barkeep looked at his rumpled and travel-stained clothing as though considering the question. He looked at the urchin and at Johan. "All we got is beef and greens. A bottle of scotch will cost you."

Johan made that alligator smile. "Fine, fine."

What Johan said to the boy Mina did not know; she had made a point of sitting on the steps in front of the saloon.

Mina wondered what he meant by "breed," as Johan had called her. She knew it meant half white and half Indian and that to be a "breed" was in some ways better than being a Negro. Yet if she was honest with herself she wasn't really certain if she had been insulted or not. With the way Johan said it she doubted it. There was a subtle difference in his treatment of her. He had taken to calling her "Ms. Mina;" a sign of respect that she appreciated. But at the same time there was no reaction to the insult in the term "nigger." It was a common enough word, but it irritated her. She doubted that he even understood the meaning, easy enough to use for many and certainly not even an insult to most. But for her the word hurt, it always had; as she knew it was no term of endearment.

She remembered Mrs. Jones; she had been so young when the grand lady had shared her thoughts about life. Those thoughts had stayed with Mina, shaped her. Take care to never treat anyone worse than you would have them treat you. Make the most of what you have, God gave it to you for a reason. Be happy with what you have because tomorrow you may not have it.

Those wise words reminded her somehow of Johan. She'd never met a man like him before. The Ma'am had been all over Europe and Mina had been with her. Gentlemen soldiers, wealthy men of commerce and society, had visited the parlor of Mrs. Jones but none had been anything like this man. His eyes, his manner were like none Mina had ever seen. She was at once frightened and intrigued by him.

Johan stood looking down at the workmen loading the boat. He absently caressed the smooth railing as he watched the deckhands load his gear into the hold. The work they were doing was not unlike some of what he had done as a youth, though those had been deep draft ocean-going ships and they had been loaded far differently than this flat-bottomed barge. But the work was the same: hard back breaking labor for little enough pay and less thanks. They were strong men of rather interesting backgrounds; he had heard accents from all over the world: Irish, Spanish, French, German, Moorish, and even a pleasant return to his childhood in the form of a Flemish accent. They were tough men used to hard physical labor who would work themselves to death for a few coin; enough for a few drinks and a meal. Some of those men would as soon as kill a man as look at him, but that was the way of the world. Those that tried to support a family on their meager earnings alone starved. Though from the way these men were built he doubted they would starve any time soon. In fact he wondered if they weren't better paid than he had been so many years ago. Last night he had watched some of these men gambling and they had lost a year's wage for a legionnaire. For men of such labor to make so much money proved that America truly was the land of opportunity.

He thought of what his boxes contained. It was little enough to show for his life. One held more clothing than he had ever owned, another cooking and camp gear, another held a tent, a crate of good tobacco and three more boxes held sundry items he hoped to trade to the Indians. His rifle, along with a pack full of clothing and other gear, sat on the feather bed in his cabin. Mina was billeted in the servant's area. He rather expected that her quarters were nowhere near as comfortable as his own. He had his own bed, clean bedding and a bath. Most importantly he had a case of good cognac to help him through the nights.

But this ride north on a riverboat was expensive, more so than he had imagined, and his money was disappearing far faster than he would have liked. At the rate he was going he would not have enough to make it as far north as Minnesota and winter there before beginning his trading with the Indian. He was going to need more money if he wanted to buy a good mule and wagon to carry his gear. He wasn't keen on changing his plan, for he thought it a good one. But necessity was a harsh mistress and she might give him no choice. He had his merchandise, he had a plan and he was prepared. What he hadn't expected was buying Mina. That had set him back more than he could really afford. He had to pay for her passage, her food and her gear as well. She said she could cook and she was a pleasure to have near by, which certainly made up for much. He might sell her… but he had promised her freedom.

He looked at his reflection in some polished brass. He was a thief, and he had murdered as well as killed before with no regrets. He rather expected he would kill and steal again. He was many things; but he was also a man who kept his word. He really had little more to show for his life than that. There would be another way to garner some monies. There were gamblers on the boat, of course, but he knew their type. He held no chance in a game with one of them, and rolling them was often as dangerous as gambling with them.

He took a pinch of tobacco and loaded his pipe as he looked out along the shore and up the bluff to the city. It wasn't unlike Sevastopol in its own way. He shuddered at that thought.

Memories of brutal cold and terrifying nights in the works washed over him. He was watching men freeze to death standing to their posts again. He had been lucky, only suffering minor frostbite on his face; others had lost fingers, toes or their very lives to the cold. Then the second day of May and the terrible assault into the teeth of the Russian defenses; Colonel Vie'not had fallen not a rifles length in front of him, his life ended by a bullet. That horrible fight with bayonets and clubbed muskets everywhere, bloody chaos. The tip of a bayonet had torn open his neck. Just a touch in any direction and that big Russian soldier would have killed him as easily as Johan had killed Kyrie's husband. But Remi had prevented it by disemboweling the man as he prepared to finish Johan. And so his own life had not been an addition to the butcher's bill paid by the Legion that day. But he still carried the scar on his neck, high up under the chin hidden by his beard.

A month and a half later they had gone forward again and there had been a far worse slaughter. Remi had been made a *Sergant chef* and he a *Sergant* simply because they were the most senior men left alive in the company. It was in the Crimea that he really learned that life meant very little, and that a bottle of cognac could chase away the worst pain and memories as well as make the cold bearable.

Johan absently rubbed at the scar on his throat as he shook his head to chase away the memories of mud and blood. Several other passengers were walking up the gangplank below him. He watched them with interest. A dozen men and several women dressed in fancy clothing. How much did just one of those dresses cost? A half dozen cases of cognac certainly or perhaps a whole wagon load? Silk and brocade with that weird tilt of the wrist to keep the hems from the mud. He smiled as one particularly rotund woman slipped and fell to her knees in the muck; several slaves and a deckhand rushed to her aid. She would have been better off in a simple dress when traveling but the wealthy never understood that. He had never understood the point of dressing up in fancy clothes; why should expensive clothing impress anyone? It was not as though a man could really work in an expensive suit. He would be afraid to stain or tear it. And one of those ladies wouldn't even think about working over a fire pit in one of those silk monstrosities.

He looked back along the deck and saw Mina sitting beside the paddle wheel on the deck below. She was sitting on a bale of fabric deftly knitting something. He had thought the request foolish; what good were balls of yarn? Yet it was the only thing she had asked from him, and so he had bought her a whole basket of the stuff. At the last minute he told her to pick out a pair of good strong boots and while she picked out a pair he got her a mirror, fancy hairpin and nicely carved wooden comb. She deserved that much thanks at least. He generally understood the words thrown about him now, though occasionally he still had to ask someone to repeat a phrase.

He watched her, those long wooden needles moving deftly in her hands. He was coming to appreciate those balls of yarn. She had made him the socks he was wearing as well as the sleeping cap and the fingerless gloves in his pack. She had made herself a wrap and was working on something else now. He hoped it was another pair of socks, as those he wore now were the most comfortable he had ever owned.

The blue she wore suited her quite well. Her long black hair was wound into a tight braid and coiled into a bun exposing her neck. He liked her; she was a good woman, gentle, and beautiful.

Johan looked back towards the shoreline and realized he wasn't the only man who appreciated the looks of Ms Mina. There was a man there in an extraordinarily expensive black silk suit and flamboyant waist coat with a fancy white silk cravat about his neck. He stood there leaning upon a silver headed walking stick, thick enough that it had to conceal steel. The man stared at Mina with a smug expression.

He was no longer young, perhaps forty, though Johan rather expected women would still think him handsome. He wore a carefully trimmed beard and sharp blue eyes stared at Mina from beneath a tall beaver skin top hat. There was obviously no real need for the fine silver headed cane. That and his bearing identified him as a dandy as well as a gentleman.

To a man like Johan, he was a victim. The way the man looked at Mina irritated him. It was akin to how men looked at horseflesh. It may well have been that he would have marked the man regardless, but that appraising look solidified his choice.

The man turned toward the gangplank, doffing his hat and offering a woman his arm. Age showed in her face and movement. While he was too far away to hear, and the noises of the boat and shore overshadowed the conversation in any case, the tone and her manner was one of complaint.

She wore her money in her clothing, a fine silk dress. She hadn't been a pretty woman in her youth and age and a lifetime of pampering had done nothing for her. Small beady eyes that he could barely tell the color of disappeared in a square unappealing face the shade of moist stone.

She wore gloves and carried a fancy parasol to keep the sun from her face. Even the parasol was silk covered with expensive lace and the handle was inlaid with both ivory and silver - worth maybe six bottles of good cognac all by itself. Johan shook his head as he descended the stairs to the deck above the gangplank so that he might better tune his ears to listen. The smug man's voice was distinctive with a strange lilt to the voice which was almost, but not quite, an English accent.

"Aunt Althea, there is no need for worry. Percy and Clara wouldn't dare run off. They have never tried before, after all. They're loyal, and you've never been overly cruel to them. Why, what would they do without you to care for them? They would starve, of course. Besides we are only going as far north as Saint Louis. You needn't worry. The abolitionists hold no sway there."

Johan smiled as he took a last pull from his pipe and knocked out the ashes. St. Louis. A lot could happen on the travel north to St. Louis. He looked at them as they ascended the stairs. The hands of the gentleman were smooth without any evidence of work. Johan nodded his head and took off his hat as he held the door for the pair of them.

"Madame and sir." Johan said with a smile; noting the fine gold watch and fat wallet in his victim's pocket as he did so.

"Thank you sir." The man smiled as he spoke and Johan detected something behind those eyes, something hidden and something dark.

As the door shut behind them he listened to the woman's shrill voice. "Too many foreigners, they are what has ruined this country. Foreigners and the abolitionists, they will bring disaster."

Mina looked over the water desperately trying to ignore the man looking at her. She quivered as she felt the man's gaze roam across her. The intense blue eyes were bad enough, but he just stood there staring! She knew he was not a gentle man from his manner. He looked at her like a he would a horse. He had stepped out of the salon; she suspected he was there gambling. She knew Johan was there as well, but she didn't think he was gambling.

She had seen this man board the boat with his aunt. Money all but dripped from them. They had come aboard with two harried-looking slaves. Mina had listened to those two gossip. Mrs. Althea was apparently a real conniving witch and the nephew a large scale slave broker hoping to start trading in Missouri.

The aged aunt had worn a fine water silk dress with no trim. such a style was intended to show off the fabric and to highlight the figure beneath. It was designed for a younger woman and did little to flatter its current wearer. The dress had to have cost a small fortune. Her parasol was almost identical to one the Ma'am had bought in Paris. Mina had always liked it because she could easily change the parasol fabric to match the dress.

Mina glanced back at the man out of the corner of her eye; he still stared at her and occasionally licked his lips.

She had heard the maid speak scornfully of the nephew who planned to buy himself "something pretty." Mina shuddered.

"Girl; who do you belong to?" His voice was somewhat shrill, like an adolescent boy.

"Monsieur Steele Sir." Mina answered quickly.

He smiled slightly. "The foreigner... those who can't, watch, I suppose."

Mina wasn't certain what he meant and didn't know if she was required to answer so she stayed silent.

The man considered a moment. "What does he drink?"

"The Monsieur drinks only the finest cognac, Sir." Mina wished he would go back inside and leave her to the stars and the sound of the river.

The man leaned closer leering at her as he did so and roughly groped her. Mina shied away from him, falling from the bale of goods and landing painfully on her rump.

The man laughed, "Quick, you are. I think I'll enjoy you very much."

Mina desperately wanted to slap the man but knew she dared not.

He looked her over again then took a swallow from his glass of whiskey. "Are you for sale?"

"No sir." She picked herself up and backed quickly away from the man.

At that moment the salon door opened and the Irish gambler, Mr. Mekennitt, stepped onto the deck. His eyes swept the scene in at a glance. His mouth pressed into a hard line and with the scar by his right eye he looked frightening in this light.

"Ahhh, Colonel Beasley. We will be starting again and it's your deal." The Irish gambler looked between the two of them and frowned.

"I had lost track of the time; thank you for fetching me." Mr. Beasely never took his eyes off Mina as he spoke.

"Girl, you're Monsieur Steele's, aren't you?" The Irishman asked.

Mina nodded. "Yes sir."

"You had best go fetch him his tobacco. I think his pouch is near to empty. I'll tell him where you went." Mina thought that pleasant Irish brogue was as close as she would ever come to hearing the voice of an angel.

She nodded that she understood and grabbed up her knitting as she hurried toward Johan's cabin. An Irishman... thank God for the Irish.

Johan stood near the tables nursing a glass of fine cognac as he watched the card game. Johan knew he was no gambler, though he could follow the cards well enough Dice were his game and even that was not a game he trusted to win him any coin. Now chess, that was a game that he enjoyed and he was a decent enough player. Though he had always been careful not to become too confident. But alas, there was precious few monies placed on such a game.

The Irish player was the master here; he was careful, and lost small when he lost at all. A dagger was tucked into his boot and the butt of a pistol protruded from his belt. Dark green eyes showed beneath the thick red hair, and a thin scar framed the edge of his right eye. Johan rather suspected the scar came from a knife. If so, the Angel of Death had glanced upon him and looked away. Professional gamblers like this one were often quite well known to the Angel of Death, as they sent her much work. This one, Sean Mekennitt, was certainly of the class of professional gambler that plied their skill up and down the rivers. Johan rather suspected he had been a soldier at one time and he had to admit that he envied the man his easy ways and friendly nature. People naturally liked and trusted the man... what had Remi called it, the gift of the Muse?

Well, whatever it was, over the years Johan had learned to only gamble upon sure things and sitting at a table with the likes of Sean Mekennitt was a far cry from a sure thing.

There were four other men at the table, all far more skilled at cards than he, and interesting sorts in their own right. There was the Creole from New Orleans, a cotton broker, the merchant on his way home to St Louis from a purchasing trip to New Orleans, and the man he had decided upon for his victim. "Colonel" William Beasley was not a careful man; he bet carelessly and lost heavily. He tossed money about easily and exuded great arrogance.

There was a thin rapier of fine Spanish steel hidden in his beautiful cane and he was quite proud of the blade showing it to all who he thought might be interested. He was a professional braggart; he reveled in speaking of his properties in land, cotton and his slaves. Johan considered just how he could take advantage of such faults.

Colonel Beasley was poor at cards, and was the sort unwilling to admit his limitations. He flaunted the wealth he wore, and was never without an expensive fitted suit, silk cravat and hand tooled boots. He had made a point of watching the porters carry his baggage aboard - and excessive and expensive luggage it had been.

For the duration of the trip north Johan had carefully listened to what the man had to say. The 'Colonel' may have been arrogant and self serving, but he was an intelligent one and a shrewd businessman. The man openly displayed his contempt for any he did not see as social equals. The man wanted for nothing, yet wanted more. He was polite, but unkind.

In some ways Johan envied the man; his education and intelligence were far beyond his own. But the other qualities, the ones he despised, had sealed the man's fate.

Johan had been only half listening to the conversation at the table when the talk of courage caught his attention. The Irishman was comparing the Comanche to the Seminoles when he was interrupted by Beasley.

"Comanches, pah! You should have seen the Highlanders make their stand at Sevastopol. Now that was a gamble of fighting men! Why there were thousands of Russians charging down that hill and the redcoats simply murdered the cowards."

The Irish gambler looked at the Colonel with a wry smile. "You were there?" Johan had always liked the Irish; they were good soldiers. Whether in the Legion or in the service of the English, they fought well.

"Of course I was. My commission was with the Black Watch; only the finest for my family." Johan had to think for a moment; a Colonel in the Black Watch...? No. He lacked the bearing; the look and attitude were all wrong for a true fighting man. He lacked even the telltale signs of a mere bandbox soldier.

Johan only half listened to the rest of the conversation. Instead he began to plan. It would have to be murder, for he had no skill for graft or the con. Blunt and brutal was what he was good at; subtlety was the purview of others. But he would have to be very careful. There were men on the decks most of the time, so disposing of a body must be well planned. He dare not let disgust or contempt cloud his judgment, or make him careless. Precision and care would be needed.

That was when he realized just how easily he had made the decision and that the plan was already there. Tonight, then. After the game.

Johan looked at the sliver of moon. The horns were indistinct; a sure sign of rain. A southbound packet boat passed them in the other channel. It had its steam up and was moving quickly, adding its own speed to the already steady current. Only a few lights showed. He looked down at the glass of Cognac in his hand and let it slosh around a little. "Seven hundred dollars. I will go no lower. She is a rare gifted woman. She knows the French almost as well as she knows the English. She would make your wife a splendid maid. I think even your aunt would approve and as you say… she is very fetching."

The man beside Johan turned his hat in his hands as he leaned against the railing. "That she is. But seven hundred dollars for a pretty house nigger. That is a bit steep even if she does know French."

Johan leaned close to the man and lowered his voice in a conspiratorial fashion. "You see I purchased her from an old woman who needed the money. A widow and she… how might you say? Was the only owner; no man."

Mr. Beasley leered. "Well now, that might just make her worth that kind of cash money. You're certain?"

Johan snorted. "I have no reason to doubt… I have not. I prefer my women… white. What is seven hundred dollars, a trifling sum, to man such as you?"

"It is a goodly sum for a house nigger; even with that figure she hides beneath those skirts. It will require a bill of sale." He straightened and put on his hat.

"Of course. I would expect nothing less. I will get it from my cabin, and you might take ownership tonight yet." Johan gave the man a knowing smile and the man smiled back. "Then we shall meet at my cabin in, say, fifteen minutes."

"No, no need, I have the money now."

"Well, then we shall go to my cabin and I shall give you the bill of sale and her papers," Johan said as he led the way toward his cabin.

The two reached his room in only a few minutes and Johan let the man in. Johan walked across his cabin setting his glass down as he did so. "Would you like some cognac?" Johan asked as he pulled a bottle from the crate. It was good strong glass, and heavy enough even though empty.

"Why yes; I think..." Johan hit him alongside the head with the bottle. The swing started at his knees and was carried through with every bit of strength Johan contained. The heavy bottle did not break, but the man did. He collapsed with a large knot and a trickle of blood on the side of his head. Quick work with a bit of cord ensured the issue.

Johan quickly stripped the man, deftly searching pockets as he went. A fine gold watch, small pistol and thick wallet in addition to the nice suit were his reward. It was too large for Johan, but he knew that he could easily sell it, and the exquisite boots too. The boots alone would bring him two bottles of cognac, and the suit another three to four. He counted the coins; fifty two gold eagles and a thick wad of paper monies. There were also two collections of papers. They looked similar to the ones that said he owned Mina. Perhaps they were the papers of the two slaves accompanying the rich aunt.

Stripping the corpse was the work of but a few minutes. Another few to be certain no one was present to see the body fall into the river, and a few seconds to pitch it into the waiting arms of the Mississippi, and the deed was done. Johan watched the body roll gently as the current took it away behind the riverboat, merely one more log floating past. It had taken so little time; less than a minute to kill the man, four to strip his body and perhaps two more to dump it in the river. Seven minutes to completely extinguish a life. How many times had he done it before or watched it done? Perhaps a dozen he had seen disposed of in similar ways, and done it himself three or four times in Amsterdam plus a time or two in the Legion.

Johan remembered the first time he had killed. The first emotion he recalled had been one of elation, pride at a job well done. The pimp who had tried to bother the Madame's house was dead and he was alive. It could have been the other way around and that would have been right for him.

He realized now just how lucky he was, that there was no hatred there. Cool, precise, impersonal emotions were the kind that killed well. For when one kills or is killed all that can be hoped for is the privilege and dignity of a swift end. Death should never be cheap, for when it became so the Angel of Death would take note of you.

Johan filled his pipe and looked at his hands. They were growing soft from his travel by train and now riverboat. When he reached Minnesota he would have to put the toughness back into them. He was going to need his hands. He lit his pipe and took a long pull. He considered his hands again; how many others had died by them, not the murders?

The memories washed over him, the swirling, choking dust and a never ending thirst. He could almost see the rocky hill with the town perched on the top and the breach they had stormed; followed by the bloody chaos of battle with bullets, bayonets and clubbed muskets against swords and rifles. How many had died there? He had to have killed a score in that god forsaken place called Ischeriden. How many more in the bone chilling cold of the Crimea and elsewhere? The memories... he felt his skin crawl and the hairs stood up on his neck as a chill went through him.

He laughed to himself at the insanity of such a thing. He was uncomfortable remembering battles where the men he tried to kill had a fighting chance. Yet he had just murdered a man in cold blood and tossed the body into the river. No remorse or regrets for that, yet almost unbearable discomfort from a distant memory?

Perhaps it was that he had *chosen* his victim; weighed and judged him, then found Beasley wanting.

He poured himself a glass of cognac; the scent of it was good and the anticipation of the taste was enough to settle his nerves.

What kind of man was he? He wasn't a murderer and thief by trade, though it came easily enough and was one of the few things he was skilled at. A life was so easy to end; a length of cord, blade or bullet all small enough things to end the life of a man all so much faster than the cholera or some other god forsaken sickness. He fully expected to fall to a bullet or knife when death came for him.

He chuckled and ran his hand through his hair; the old Voyageur had told him some of the Red Indian tribes scalped the dead. Perhaps that would be how it would end for him. Yes, he would like that; a final hard fought battle where he sold himself dearly. He could not see himself passing in a feather bed, for he hadn't lived that way and so that could not be the way he went.

He steadily puffed on his pipe as he considered the documents on the small table in front of him. The papers were almost identical to the ones he held that declared him the owner of Mina. What were the names he had overheard? Percy and Clara? That seemed right. Had Mina met them? He would need her in the morning. While he could write his own name and could recognize it on the rolls, he could read little more than that. She could tell him exactly what he had and he might tell her his plan. Johan chuckled; he was a real bastard, a real no doubt about it villain. What was the name of that book Remi had read aloud in the barracks? The *Count of Monte Cristo,* that was it, by the Frenchman Dumas. But which villain was he? He certainly was not the Count, though he liked the way the man had worked.

How did the ownership of a slave work? Was it as simple as possession of the papers? No, there must be more to it than that. What if Mina delivered their papers to the two slaves? Would they be intelligent enough to make a break for freedom? The wealthy Aunt Althea would protest... but what if he provided a forged bill of sale? There were many possibilities and he would explore them all.

Johan emptied his glass then cleaned his pipe and crawled into bed. He stared up at the ceiling and wondered what the morning would bring him. A good deed perhaps. Not that the old woman would call it good. He smiled. Perhaps God would use tomorrow to cross out one of his evils.

He rolled onto his side and embraced glorious sleep.

Minnesota

Minnesota was a new state, a place of cheap and bountiful land. A man or family willing to work hard could accomplish much, and build a future. Thus it became the ultimate destination for many immigrants.

Seth looked up the hill to where the new man stood next to the wood pile. He was one of the hundreds of immigrants coming up the river and he had brought his woman, a Negress. Seth had to think a moment to remember the names of the other three or four black people he had seen. At first he had thought the woman the man's slave, but it took only a moment or two of watching the two of them together to know that wasn't so.

Then too, Father would never have hired a man who owned slaves. Father had supposed that the new man had brought the woman with him from abroad. After all, the two of them spoke French at least as often as they spoke English. Their accents were interesting; when Mina spoke it was with a pleasant drawl not unlike a southern twang. But Johan didn't speak with the familiar Swede or Norwegian accent that was so common. No, it was different and Seth didn't care for it.

Were the two really married, though? He hoped not, as Mina was a fine looking woman and an incredible cook as well as a competent seamstress. Though Seth had no doubt mother would never approve of him courting a colored woman - that would shame her more than if he chose to court an Indian girl.

Even if not for his mother's disapproval, though, Seth could not have pursued Mina. In his heart, he knew the two were wed. They had to be. Father would never have allowed a couple living in sin to work for him. He was tolerant, but there were some things that were just too much for his sensibilities.

Still, they were welcome. Johan was a man willing to work when told to do so and he seemed to enjoy that work. He had some skill with an ax and had an idea of how to use mules. He wasn't particularly *skilled* with anything, but he was willing to learn, quick in some ways, slower in others. And Seth had to admit that the man never admitted defeat. Mother, naturally, appreciated Mina. She was hard-working and willing to help with anything. But even more importantly, his little sister Carlie liked the woman. The two talked constantly of fashion as they worked together in the laundry and kitchen.

Seth still wasn't really sure what he thought of Johan. For sure, both the other hired men were nervous around him, and Corwin was certain Father had hired the man as a sort of foreman. The boy smiled to himself at the thought of Father needing a foreman. Though slow to anger - Seth couldn't remember seeing Father truly furious more than twice - foolish indeed would be the man who tested his temper!

Johann had brought so much gear with them. Seth was not really sure what it all was, but there was a cart full of it. He half-wondered if he should sneak a look inside to make certain Father wasn't taking in a thief. There was something to the man that Seth didn't quite trust, something cold in the man's eyes that bothered him. Father had always been an excellent judge of character. He'd always been able to avoid the random waste-abouts, hiring instead the men who were willing to work.

Maybe that was it. Other hired hands had always been good, God-fearing Christian men who were comfortable in their faith. But this man, Seth wasn't even sure believed. Oh, he listened to the prayers and lowered his head and clasped his hands at all of the right times but there was something missing... something Seth just couldn't quite place. And he definitely didn't care for the way Johan looked at his mother and sister; too appraising. Though, in fairness, he looked at his woman in the same way, and a bit more often.

Father had said the man carried himself like a professional soldier, yet Seth wondered about that. Why would a soldier come to the frontier and not join the Army? It made no sense to him. Soldiers were needed out west against the Sioux and Dakota, not here.

Oh, what a glorious life to carry a sword and fight in fantastic battles as written of by Sir Walter Scott! That was the kind of life that interested Seth. He loved the stories of the Wars with Napoleon and the Crusades. His imagination supplied such glorious images! Exciting battles and victories, with wonderful parades through the heart of a city, and adoring girls at the end - *that* was the life of a soldier!

It promised so much more. Adventure and excitement instead of the boring life on the farm. Maybe he could get a story or two from Johan about War and Adventure; that might be neat. Perhaps at supper tonight he would get him to talk about it.

The rifle the man favored was pretty nice too; Father had called it 'the weapon of a soldier.' Though Seth knew Father loved his Colt revolving rifle, there was an instant appreciation of that Windsor.

Seth still preferred his old squirrel rifle. It was smaller and handier, and he knew he could hit anything he needed to with it. The rifling always carried his patched round ball right where he pointed it, and no one ever had complained about the rabbits, raccoon or squirrels he had handed mother for the stew pot.

He had often pretended a Sioux warrior had been on the other side of his sight instead of a squirrel or rabbit. Would he, could he, really pull the trigger if a man was to be on the receiving end of that .36 caliber ball?

Yes, of course he would. If the time ever came, he would do his duty protecting the family. Father had always stressed that when the time came to defend the homestead there would be no time to ponder the morality of killing a man.

He knew Father had asked Johan that if Indians attacked the place would he be willing to fight to defend it. His answer had been quite revealing. "I have fought before. I expect I will have to again." That had been enough for Father, but Seth wanted to know more. He wished Father would have pushed him for more information, but regardless of any doubts he might have, this fellow Johan and his woman were worth the two dollars a week plus room and board that Father was paying them.

Johan breathed in the aroma of fresh baked bread as he looked through the kitchen window. He smiled as Mina and Mrs. Barnaby worked around the stove. Mina moved about the place with plates while Mrs. Barnaby stirred dinner. The woman knew what she was about in a kitchen; she might have been beautiful in her youth and she was still a striking woman. Black hair and dark eyes with near perfect features made her the kind of woman he took notice of. Her daughter Carlie was a younger version of her mother, maybe fifteen and rapidly growing to a beauty as well. Carlie was like a butterfly, always flitting from one interest to the next, never quite settling for what she saw. She would shatter many a heart before she settled on a man, but she would likely make that man eternally happy. Johan grinned as he watched her walk into the kitchen with a basin of water to help her mother and Mina.

It was amusing really; three very lovely women in one house. He chuckled. He was not a particular man and he would have gladly accepted any of them into his bed. Not that he really expected that any was likely to invite him. He was not that kind of man.

Come to think of it, he had always paid for sex in some way. Part of that might have come from his youth in the brothel. The idea of not paying for it seemed odd. And the idea of prostitution was not all that bad to him. For most of the women he had known, there had been few other options.

He shook himself from the thought of brothels and looked to the sky; it was so clear. Not unlike the desert sky, with occasional white clouds that provided bits of cool shade. He liked a sky without the smoke from houses and factories to stain it. There was so much of it above his head; it was everything that he had been told. This Minnesota sky held the whole world.

Johan listened to the wind whistling through the trees rustling the leaves as it whispered to him on the way by. He enjoyed the riot of color presented by the fall leaves, and it was a sight he would always appreciate. He could remember nothing like it in the old world and certainly nothing like it in Africa.

He looked back at the house. It was strongly built of stout gray field stones that would help weather the seasons with ease. This one had a dozen windows, and that alone made it a grand house to him. It was snug and well built, the size of a barracks, and Johan had certainly lived in smaller ones. The house was well planned out with three rooms plus a kitchen, porch and mudroom on the main floor with three large bedrooms on the second.

The barn was enormous, big enough to sleep most of the old Second Regiment. There were stalls for cattle and a dozen horses as well as a store room and workshop with plenty of room for his cart and the merchandise he hoped to trade with the Indians.

Johan looked at the well house, above which he and Mina slept. He liked it very much. It was small and snug, sturdily built of the same materials as the house. And the bed he slept in was very comfortable, a real improvement over the years of sleeping on the ground or a pair of boards with a bit of bedding. Mina didn't complain about the bed either. Was it an improvement over what she had known in Charleston?

He turned and looked to the south side of the hill to the carriage house, above which the other two hired hands slept. It was as well built as the rest of the buildings, though the only stone in the construction was the foundation. Good heavy board and timber construction, the stable was also built to last. Mr. Barnaby was a man who thought of the future and who wasn't above putting some serious work into that future. Johan admitted he liked and admired the man; any man who could build what he had in only a few years deserved respect.

It was a good family that lived here, a good man and his family. He shook his head as he imagined the wealth that had built this place. Mr. Barnaby had said he and his son with some hired help had come to this place with little more than a wagon and some stock. In three years they had built the house and barn, living in the cave below the well house until the house was done. They had finished the carriage house only last year. Johan marveled at their dedication and effort put forth here. He respected men like that and wished he was one of them.

Johan turned and looked at the young man named Seth walking up from the barn. He had to admit he liked the boy. He was a smart one and certainly looked the son of the man who had built this place, and had much of the same sound to his voice. Though he was only sixteen or so he was already grown in build, though not yet in mind and heart; he was more than a little naïve.

"Johan, thanks for your help pulling down those trees and trimming them. Father thinks they'll work pretty fair for the new pole shed. You already cleaned up for dinner?" His manner irritated Johan a little bit. Seth was young, but he was not small. His powerful shoulders, big hands and the easy way about him proved that the boy was every bit the hard worker of Johan and the other two hired men. But he still seemed to look up to the hired hands, and deferred to them as though they were in charge. Seth was no leader and would have to change his manner if he ever hoped to take over from his father. If he failed to stop deferring, he would find men constantly taking advantage of him.

Mr. Barnaby came out of the privy below the house, the door banging shut behind him, and walked towards them. Barnaby kept his face clean shaven, but there was the perpetual shadow of a beard. Johan was not certain if women would think him handsome or not. Though Johan suspected the other man was not that much older than he, there were streaks of grey in his blond hair and his blue eyes were those of an old man. Despite those marks of age, he was spry and quick, and from his actions around the mules and other livestock Johan knew he was a man who understood animals.

"Seth, Johan, you two ready for supper? Johan, you and Seth will need to split some wood after dinner if you aren't too tuckered out."

Johan smiled, "Yes sir. I will be quite ready for more work after we eat. I think the women have made a good dinner; it smells such."

Mr. Barnaby led his son and Johan into the snug house with the other hired men coming in soon after as they finished washing up. The fragrances in the house where overwhelming; fresh bread and the alluring smell of venison stew. Johan stopped and inhaled deeply then let out a sigh of pleasure. Seth grinned and Mr. Barnaby laughed.

"The wife is the best cook in this part of the country. Of course I might be a touch biased." Mr. Barnaby directed a crooked grin at his wife.

The woman really was the mother of Seth and Carlie; there could be no doubt about it when they stood close together. The family resemblance was uncanny. All shared the same eyes and same cheekbones. Though, Carlie had shown a mischievous streak that could only have come from her father.

Mr. Barnaby moved to the head of the large and ornate oaken table and took his place at the head. Seth sat beside him. Oscar and Corwin, the other hired men, sat down as well. Johan paused a moment then sat down. All three ladies brought forth the food and placed it on the table. A jar of pickled tomatoes, a loaf of still- warm bread and a large pot full of fresh stew. Johan could smell the venison and could see bits of carrot, cabbage and turnips floating in the pot. Oh, how he loved a good meal, and this promised to be another excellent one. Johan could fairly feel his mouth watering as Carlie dished out the stew.

As the ladies sat down and passed around the pickles and bread Johan looked at the two hired men. He liked them both; hard working young men who appreciated the value of a good wage, nice room and good food in payment for their labor. Corwin was an artist with an ax or an adze who could drop and trim a tree with minimal effort. His big brawny build and face that seemed to be chiseled from stone garnered him many an appreciative look from the women in town and Johan had heard him talking of the woman he was courting, a pretty Norwegian named Eva.

Oscar lacked the looks and powerful build of Corwin but the man knew how to use a crosscut saw and had a way with the livestock that seemed almost magical to Johan. He had but to speak in that deep baritone voice of his and the cattle, horse and mules took note. He had no need to curse the working stocks, they willingly responded to his voice. That would probably have gotten him branded as some sort of witch in the Legion. Johan grinned at the thought; he had certainly never seen anything like it before.

By now Johan knew the routine. He dare not dive into his food until the prayers were said. That did not stop his mind from reaching out and tasting it though. Everyone clasped hands with their neighbors and lowered their heads in an attitude of prayer.

The man of the house spoke with a voice that resonated throughout the room. "Bless us, o Lord, for these thy gifts which we are about to receive, and thy bounty; through Christ our Lord.

"Lord, Thank you for the hands that made us this feast and for the hands that made this food possible; thank you for the health and wealth you have granted the men and women brought to this table.

"May your kindness and mercy never drift from this family and all they touch; please watch over and grant wisdom to the leaders of this land and help them to do what is right and true. Amen." As the prayer finished all kept their heads bowed a moment longer to add their own prayers and then dove into the food as though there were no tomorrow.

No words or conversation beyond a "Please pass the salt," or a "Might I have some more stew?" emerged from the men and women around the table for some time. Eating was serious work, not to be undertaken lightly and it brooked few interruptions.

"I believe you to have been a soldier, is this right?" Seth asked.

"*Oui*- I mean, yes that is true." Johan said as he sopped up the last of his stew with a scrap of bread, and added cautiously, "I was in the French Army."

Mr. Barnaby considered a moment. "Might I ask where?"

Johan looked at the man. "North Africa, the Crimea and back to North Africa."

Seth looked excited. "The Crimea, the land of the *Charge of the Light Brigade*, did you see it happen?"

"No, I was in the trenches in front of Sevastopol." Johan said, feeling ice creep into his words.

"What was it like?" Seth asked as he leaned forward with an eager look on his face.

Johan looked at the boy; he was so young. He had no idea of the horror of war. He had likely read books or listened to some old liar brag about his experiences in some battle or another. He could have no idea, no concept of the ugliness. Johan had seen too many young men like this one end their days in some Crimean grave. "How do I tell you of the absolute horror of it?" he said finally. "Should I talk first of Turk who froze to death on sentry duty or of my friend Maurice who was bayoneted in the belly and lived through three days of agony before the Angel of Death finally took him? Perhaps I could speak of watching blood turn to ice before it could soak into the earth. Then I think I would speak of the Cholera and dysentery killing more of my friends than the Russians. No, I think I should give you the tale of how I made *Sergent*; I and my *copain*, Remi, were the only men in the company left to report for duty. We were the veterans to the new men. We watched too many die so we learned to make friends of no man lest we mourn over much when they fell. The Angel of Death was quite busy and the gentlemen generals made her work easy." Johan spoke coldly; the memories rising to the surface and cutting into him like knives. He needed cognac, something to push the memories back.

For a moment the entire table was silent. Mina had a hand up to cover her mouth. Carlie and Mrs. Barnaby both looked frightened, possibly by the look on his face. The others simply stared at Johan. They did not understand; they could not. For them war was something glorious, not the horror Johan spoke of.

"I lost many friends there. Might we speak of something else?" he said then. He had no wish to ruin the evening.

Mr. Barnaby cleared his throat. "Johan, you are recently come from the east and a recent addition to our fair country." As he spoke he set aside his empty plate. "I believe I overheard Ms. Mina say that the two of you boarded a boat north at Vicksburg."

Again, Mr. Barnaby was not asking a question, so Johan merely nodded his agreement instead of speaking as he leaned back in his chair.

"What did you think of slavery?" The question was a welcome change of subject. It was also a bit of a surprise.

68

"I did not care for it. But I have seen slave markets before." Johan was not certain where Mr. Barnaby was going with this. Did he suspect something was amiss with Mina?

"What do you think should be done with slavery?"

"I do not know. You Americans seem to have found a solution by keeping half the country free of slavery. It seems to work here in America." Still uncertain what Mr. Barnaby wanted, Johan spoke carefully.

"No, it should be destroyed. Either bought out like the British did, or abolished as in Russia." Mr. Barnaby grew very quiet and looked hard at all those around the table. No one spoke or moved. "When we see something wrong we should try to make it right!" He banged his fist against the table for emphasis. "It isn't enough to silently condemn evil or to congratulate ourselves for not participating. There is an obligation to stand against it."

Corwin and Oscar both nodded their heads in agreement and Seth uttered a quiet "Amen."

"It will get many men killed. Those I saw in the South will not let their slaves go easily." Johan said.

"How long can one watch evil and do nothing about it? How long can this nation remain half free and half slave?" Mr. Barnaby fairly thundered.

Johan grimaced. "It will take a war, I think, to free the slave in this country and even then little will change. There is too much money in slavery."

Mr. Barnaby looked hard at Johan. "How do you say that? The men of the South are good God-fearing men; they have but to look at the Bible to know that it is an evil."

"Aye and they can look to the Bible and find excuses for slavery as well. It is too much money; many thousands of dollars in property and that is all they will see. I do not believe they see a slave as a man or a woman, but as property. As you see your cattle and horses, so they see the slave. It is the same elsewhere. Slaves here, though, are much more expensive and because of that they are worth more." Johan wasn't exactly sure that he was right; but it was what he had seen in his short travel west from Charleston and in his encounter with Mr. Beasley.

"But you think a war is what it will take? No, we are all Americans we cannot fight other Americans. Though... if you do turn out to be right, who will you side with?"

Johan's reply was simple and gained a look from everyone at the table. "I shall side the army of freedom."

Mina dipped her hands into the scalding water and pulled out a plate. Some quick work with the scrub brush and a wipe with the wash rag and she handed it to Carlie. Carlie dipped it in the rinse water and set it on the drying rack. It was simple monotonous work that was there every day, three times a day. There would never be an end to it. It wasn't really the kind of work she enjoyed, preferring her knitting, sewing or making bread. But it was good work to be doing when the spirit and mind were troubled.

These people were so different than what she had known in Charleston. Six months ago she had been a wealthy widow's slave, and now here she was doing housework beside white people. And they were white people who almost treated her as an equal. Carlie behaved more like a sister, and the rest of the family offered her a quiet dignity she had never experienced from white folk. She was not really certain how to react to such.

Johan had told her to say she was from Marsielle in France via Charleston. He had said: "You are no longer a slave, you are my wife. Or if you would prefer, you may call yourself my ward."

He had given her a choice; it wasn't much of one but he had given it. And he hadn't touched her... Mina felt herself blush; at least not in *that* sense.

She looked at Carlie a moment. She didn't like to lie to the girl, but maybe she wasn't when she called Johan her husband. Johan was hers. At least, that was how she looked at it, so why not call him her husband? There had been no service of any kind and she rather doubted there ever would be one. That they had called each other husband and wife was enough.

Their first night here... she smiled slightly, faintly. Johan had dropped his bedroll to the floor! She hadn't been really quite sure what to say, so she'd simply pulled aside the covers and pointed to the bed.

He'd grunted and crawled in between the sheets and went to sleep. She had expected him to touch her, to hold her. She'd told herself to be ready for the unexpected and when he did nothing she was almost angry at him. He'd just gone to sleep!

She had to admit she'd thought of smothering him for that. She'd even gone so far as to plan it out. She had never shared a bed with anyone but the Ma'am and that didn't count. All sorts of romantic notions had been in her head, but they had been shattered by the simple action of his closed eyes and shallow even breathing. He hadn't even touched her! With a slight headshake, she looked out the window at Johan splitting wood. He was a strange man, still, but he was *her* strange man.

The conversation at tonight's supper had been interesting, to say the least. The pain and rage that she had seen in Johan's gaze... His eyes had actually changed color and the look on his face was impossible to describe, but she would never forget it. It had frightened her in a way she had never been frightened before.

Carlie playfully splashed her with a bit of the rinse water. "What are you thinking about? Pass me the next plate."

Carlie was so pretty; Mina could imagine her strolling the Charleston battery in a fine dress the envy of every man. "I... was just thinking what kind of dress I could make you with that green fabric your mother has in the sewing room." Her lie was easy and small; hardly a sin.

Carlie grinned her nose crinkling as she did so. "Liar! I saw you blush when you were staring at your husband. What were you thinking about?"

"About my husband," Mina said with a sly smile.

Carlie chuckled. "You are a naughty woman, Mina!"

Mina felt herself blush further. "Not like that! I was thinking what a strange man he can be."

Carlie cocked her head to one side and looked at her carefully. "I think I know what you mean. He really frightened mother tonight. His words were so... hard?"

"I know. Like he was talking to us from the past, like it was right in front of him. He's never spoken of it to me."

"Really? I would have thought the two of you held no secrets from one another."

"It's not that. I knew he had been in the army. He just has never spoken of it."

Carlie looked out the window at Johan as she swirled a plate in the rinse water. "Oh. Father talked about the scars some men carry and that we should not speak of it again to him." Disappointment was evident in her voice.

Mina thought about the scars she had seen on Johan. There was one low down on his left side, one right on top of a rib and another on his throat under his beard; the hair grew different there. She had wondered about them but never asked. "Mr. Barnaby is right, I think. Some men don't speak of what they have experienced... they know we cannot understand."

"I bet he was an officer..."

"No, he was no officer, but a common soldier." Mina didn't know why she said it or even how she knew it, but of that fact she was certain.

Carlie absently stacked another dish onto the rack. "How did you meet him?"

Mina looked at her a moment. "It was at the market."

"Was it love at first sight?" Carlie asked with a wicked grin.

Mina laughed and thought for a moment. "No, I think it was when I was teaching him English."

"Tell me about it; I want to fall in love one day." Carlie spoke with a wistfulness that made Mina smile.

Raise the splitting maul, let it fall and toss the split wood onto the pile or set it back up to split again. Johan worked the pile of firewood. He enjoyed the smooth feel of the well worn handle in his hands. He had always enjoyed cutting wood, splitting firewood or making kindling. Such work had always given him a sense of calm. He enjoyed knowing that his labors would warm or feed the cook fire that would feed him. Over the years he had helped split fence rail, and had tried his hand at shingle making. He lacked the skill for the second, though it was one he wished was his. He had always wanted to build something he could be proud of, something like this farmstead, but he had always lacked the skill.

Adding to the woodpile was the kind of work that allowed a man to think, and the dinner conversation of slavery had been of that kind. It seemed to be so every evening. Last night Mr. Barnaby had spoken at length with Corwin about the free public schools and the importance of education. The night before that, he and Seth had argued about the need for a large standing army. Every night a different subject of conversation; every night Johan listened, learned and wondered.

He glanced to the massive stack of wood nearby. He and the others had dragged all of the deadfalls out of the draw and hillside above the house. Though he knew he shouldn't have been, he was surprised how all of the men knew every kind of wood they touched and what it would be best used for. These men lived and worked with every kind of timber, so there really was no reason they *shouldn't* know what kind of wood they were dealing with. He envied them their knowledge and the usefulness of that knowledge. There were better than sixty trees down that they were going to use. The trimmings would make a good supply of hinges, hooks, springs and the scraps kindling and firewood. Combined with the dead falls they were dragging out of the timber, it was a good supply that would go a long way toward feeding the stoves in the house, well house and carriage house for the winter. Oscar and Corwin had finished stacking hay into the barn and were washing up below the well house. It had been a long hard day and they would all likely sleep well tonight.

They had already harvested a field worth of corn and it resided in an odd building with only slatted walls and a roof. Most of it would go toward feed for the horses and other stock. Johan had spent the last several evenings busily replacing nails in the carriage house with wooden pegs so the tack hung upon them would last longer. It was a trick he had learned from the Legion and it was simple enough to do.

Johan split the last chunk and looked to Seth, who was piling the split firewood into a neat stack that made a decent wall below the house. There were perhaps ten cords of wood already stacked there. It was a lot of wood, enough to feed the stoves in the house, carriage house and well house – for a while at least. He had been warned that the Minnesota winter would be cold; but compared to the Crimea, at least here he would have a roof over his head and a stove with ample wood to shelter him from the bitter wind.

Johan put down the splitting maul and took a long stretch. His muscles ached from the work of the day but it felt good. He and the others had accomplished a good bit today; trimming and hauling down a score of good straight poles. He liked the work of splitting wood and building walls of firewood that would be used in the stoves of the homestead. Tomorrow they were going to spend the day splitting shingles for the roof.

Room and board in exchange for a winter's worth of work. The deal was fair, and though the work was hard it was satisfying. And at least he was not spending money on living. When he left to trade in the spring, he would still have some monies left and would be in good physical condition.

It was a bit strange; he had been warned several times about the Minnesota winter, but found himself almost looking forward to it. He had not seen any real snow since the Crimea, and Seth's questions had brought those memories to the fore of his mind. There was something pure and beautiful about a world covered in a silent white blanket. So he was no stranger to chill weather. He had long ago learned how to cope with and survive it. But this would be his first where he actually controlled his own destiny; the first winter in a truly new life.

September 1860, Dakota Territory

In 1860 the northern frontier was the area we know today as North and South Dakota. It was a land of opportunity for an ambitious and active man willing to risk trading with the Dakota, Lakota and other plains tribes. Many of the tribes who were distrustful of the United States preferred to deal with the French. French Voyageurs had traded with the plains tribes for generations and many had become very wealthy doing so.

Mina let her mind wander. Would she would ever forget the months since they had left the Barnaby farm.? The wide open sky, and the land so clear you could see to the end of the world... they stayed with you. Some people feared tight places, close spaces. Did some people also fear no end of sky or not seeing trees for days on end? The wind talked to you out on these plains, whispered secrets to you. The wind told her when Johan snuck a sip from his cognac or watched her sleep. She loved the feel of the wind in her face, caressing her cheeks and playfully mussing her hair. But above all she loved Johan's touch, his soft caress.

It amazed her that Johan's rough hands could be so gentle as they rubbed the weariness out of her neck or gently ran his hands through her hair. He was always gentle with her. His voice was always soft, never sharp or angry when he spoke to her.

She had watched Johan learn out on these plains. He was a careful student. He had taught himself how to track an animal across the plains, to make a smaller fire, to walk with God. But did he know God walked with him? She didn't think so; he was not a pious man. Though... occasionally there was a spirit in his actions and words that spoke to her and made her wonder.

She had taught him English and how to listen. Her only failing with him was in teaching him to read. He lacked the patience and would get quickly frustrated, calling the writing bird scratchings that made no sense to him.

He was little different than most white men... or was he? She didn't know any other white man the way she did him... and she didn't want to, white or otherwise! This one was hers; she had taught him, claimed him as her own. He had taken her from civilization out to the ends of the earth, to the land of the Lakota, and treated her like a human being.

Mina could see that he appreciated and admired the Lakota people, the warriors in particular. He was a strange man, her Johan, always on the outside looking in and wishing to belong but never expecting to. He had a need to be needed. She wasn't sure she could quite understand that, but she was willing to accept it.

He had taught her so much in the last year. Now she could start a fire with a bit of lint and a flint and steel. She could pack things so efficiently that there was always extra room in the cart. She had learned to make the ingredients of one meal stretch to make four. But that was only the least of what she had learned; she had learned to love the man and to appreciate him.

When had that happened? She wasn't certain, either when or really how. It wasn't as if he were truly handsome. as looks went he was quite plain in her eyes. He had a good spirit; she could see it. Though, there were times when she wondered where that spirit was. He was a simple man, with simple ideas of right and wrong. Any who were willing to do what he did were his equals. Those who were too good for work were below his contempt. At times he was loud and outspoken, but for the most part he simply watched, listened and learned. He was careful, more so away from the towns. People didn't surprise him out here but she thought they likely irritated him in the settlements. He was often curt and short with people, yet there were times he seemed to be genuinely appreciative of the efforts of someone… usually her. She wasn't certain what he had done that made her love him. But it didn't really matter that much. She had come to love him for who he was.

She had started to learn the man at the Barnaby place last winter and then upon the plains she had come to understand him, at least as far as a woman could understand a man. He hadn't told her she was to come west into the Indian lands with him; he had asked. He had even offered to have her stay at the Barnaby homestead. She could have. She liked working there, and considered Carlie her friend... but being there without Johan was unthinkable. She wanted to be beside him, to live with him and to love him, forever. His near presence made her feel safe, appreciated and loved. No one else had ever made her feel like that, only her Johan.

Mina had never thought of herself as pretty, but first Johan and then the Lakota men had changed her mind. She must have been something to look upon if Johan always treated her as a lady and one handsome Lakota boy had offered Johan four beautiful horses in trade for her. But Johan had refused... called her his woman, but not his to sell. That alone was something. *Not his to sell.* She liked that. She would write about that in her new memory book when they stopped.

She liked the Lakota people; their inherent humor and their view of life. They were so different than anything she had ever even imagined. That difference made them almost beautiful to her. Simple lodges they called a tepee , and their only possessions were what could be carried by a pony with a travois. They led a simple but hard life. She knew Johan thought them great fighting men, and she suspected he wished he was one of them. He liked and appreciated such a life; but she also knew he had liked life at the Barnaby place, with the tight roof and solid walls, and he respected what Mr. Barnaby had accomplished in carving the farm from the land.

Johan felt the cool wind on his face and listened to the approaching horsemen. He had half expected Cheif Bald

Eagle's boy to come and take Mina, but these weren't Lakota, or any of the other tribes he had dealt with. The hoofbeats were different, heavier and more distinctive. These were shod horses, and shod hooves meant white men.

Well, if they were bent upon mischief then life would likely be very short, and he did not doubt there would be at least two less white men in the world. Mina had the shotgun, and he had a round loaded in his rifle. He considered the last several months as he watched to see what manner of men would crest the ridge.

The Lakota were a strong people, not unlike the Kabyle warriors he had fought in North Africa. He rather expected they were every bit as self-sufficient, if not a bit more so. Given how the men looked, they were a hard-fighting, dangerous and skilled foe - the kind of men he respected. Perhaps half of the warriors in the bands he had dealt with carried rifles or muskets, while the rest carried a mix of bows and lances. Most of the long arms he saw had been cut down or shortened, for these were a people who preferred close combat. Fighting and killing an enemy while looking him in the eye was what they preferred, and that was as it should be.

In his youth he had preferred the knife, but the Legion had taught him to use the musket and the bayonet. He had become a master with the bayonet; Remi had called him an artist. Later he learned to shoot a rifle, to truly hunt men. He had taken to the rifle very well, but he missed looking into the eyes of a man about to die. The rifle gave a detached quality that was not comfortable. Fighting and killing was what he had always been good at.

He almost enjoyed a good fight, though he was not such a fool as to believe he was invincible. That was the kind of attitude that brought one to the attention of the Angel of

81

Death and when she took notice of you the end was near. The Lakota favored the close-in fight; eye to eye where man might measure man. It meant more than a bullet from nowhere. The only mercy a soldier should ever expect was a swift end, and in that sense the bullet was the right tool. But he would rather send a man to the Angel of Death via the bayonet, somehow it seemed more respectful. A bullet from out of sight was close to cold blooded murder.

For the most part the Lakota disdained anything longer ranged than their short bows. The sudden shock of an ambush or cavalry charge appeared to be their style. They were warriors of the highest order. Johan respected them for that, even as he thought of how best to fight them. Infantry could never bring them to battle except on their own terms, and those terms would not likely be to the advantage of the infantry. Using cavalry against them would be no easier task as they knew the land and how to use it to their advantage. Johan wouldn't be willing to put any coin on the outcome of a fight against them. More often than not he suspected the Lakota would come out ahead.

The chief he had met, Bald Eagle, was an old warrior, one who had seen the sharp end of life and death many times. But though he looked eighty, with hard-beaten lines on his face that reminded Johan of a map, the spirit of a young man still resided within him, his physique and muscles proving him to be no worse off than a boy of twenty. And the men who followed him were fighting men of a kind that would bring fear to the throat of any soldier. Bald Eagle's oldest son had reminded him of Remi, and his youngest... a young Remi. Fighting men that did not know the meaning of defeat were men he would rather serve beside than fight.

The Lakota he had dealt with were an inherently honest people when dealing with their friends and allies; but to those they called enemy there was not a more ruthless or deadly adversary. The garrisons built by the US Army to defend the frontier were lightly manned and too thinly spread to deter these people if they opted for war. A lot of people would pay for such an oversight. Still, the soldiers of the US Army were not the only fighting men along the frontier. Every white man and woman had best be well armed and capable of defending themselves, for the Lakota and their allies were not a people that differentiated between civilian and soldier. The Lakota were little different from the Tauregs and Kabyle warriors he had faced… men, women and children were all enemies that the knife or bullet dealt with equally.

These were a people who expected no quarter and gave none. He did not think them evil, as he had heard some say they were. They were fighting men with little respect for those who were not. Johan understood their view; was it wrong? *He* certainly was not the man to make such a judgment, as he rather suspected that God would treat him rather harshly for his own actions in life.

The Lakota he had dealt with had been fair in their dealings with him; trading furs for his steel pots and pans and accepting his knives as worthy gifts. The old Voyageur had told him to give a small twist of tobacco to every chief as a gift to open any trading. That had been worthy advice which had served him well. His other gifts were small patch knives, sturdy and sharp and had opened many trades over the last six months. Those knives had been a good investment, as well as a wise decision to use as gifts, for with every knife he had gifted, he received a pelt of some sort in return. The cart was full to overflowing with all kinds of animal skins.

Some of those concerned him. He couldn't identify all of them. Rabbit were easily recognized, but others could be squirrel or maybe even rat, and for all he knew could be worthless. Of course, the buffalo hides he had traded for would be worth their weight in gold; heavy, thick and warm, they would bring far more than the best wool blanket. Johan hoped he might make a tidy profit selling them in St Paul or one of the settlements along the Mississippi. He would have liked to winter at the Barnaby homestead again, but felt it better to stay closer to St Paul where his money might go further; and where he might replenish his stock of cognac.

Johan looked at Mina crouching with that shotgun in the mule cart, the wind disturbing her thick hair. One of Chief Bald Eagle's sons had offered him four good horses for her. The young man was quite taken with her, as was Johan. Though it was not at all the normal or common thing, he knew he treated her more as a friend and wife than as any servant. Whether over a stove or an open fire she was a rare fine cook, but there was more to it than her cooking. She was a truly good woman and he liked her very much… no, he had come to love her.

He watched the first men crest the ridge. Cavalry, less than a quarter of a mile away and the column was turned towards him. They were well mounted on fine corn-fed horses. Johan squinted, focusing on the men. Each carried a pistol and carbine, but only the officer carried a saber. Not a surprise. The sword would not be a particularly effective weapon out here on the plains. Most sat their horses comfortably in the manner of men who spent long hours in the saddle, and their carbines were carried at the ready. They looked surprisingly competent, but were a different manner of soldier than the Hussars and Cuirassiers that he was used to seeing. There was no flash, no pretty buttons and lace, only cold efficiency. He would not have wanted to face this kind of light cavalry on the field of battle, and they were likely the only kind that could hope to deal with warriors the like of the Lakota. He set his hammer to half cock and relaxed slightly. There shouldn't be trouble here.

A young officer with a pair of enlisted men and a sergeant left the formation and galloped toward him. It was interesting to watch them move. The Sergeant and two enlisted rode their mounts in the manner of a men trained into the saddle. The officer rode as a man likely to end the march with a set of saddle sores. What a contrast it was to the Lakota or Tauregs! Those were men born into the saddle. These men were not so fluid; though they were clearly veteran fighting men, they were not the expert horsemen of the Lakota. Still, they would be dangerous foes to Chief Bald Eagle and his warriors.

The officer rode up and reined his horse in sharply, coating Johan with a small cloud of dust. Johan scowled at the fool as he coughed away the dust that settled into his nostrils. The rude little bastard had had no need to do that.

"You, civilian; you came from the west?" The Lieutenant was more than a touch arrogant and he was young; obviously a recent addition to the frontier. A small, almost pinched face with close set blue eyes over a large mustache gave him a distinctive look. But the mustache did not suit his face well. It was too obviously an attempt to look older. A woman might have thought him to have been handsome but the first impression he gave Johan was that of an effete dandy.

Johan turned and looked at the obvious wheel ruts in the grass. "*Oui*. I have spent the summer trading with the Lakota." Johan looked at the small column of men and their rather obvious trail. "You must have come from Fort Abercrombie."

"You have had business with the red savage?" The Lieutenant was looking past him to his cart and Mina. "Where are you from?"

"I trade furs where I please and am from many places. Currently the Minnesota, St Paul," Johan replied curtly. "And a good afternoon to you as well."

Johan cradled his rifle in his arm and let part of his gaze travel to the squad of cavalry, and then back to focus on the Sergeant. He was a massive man who carried himself with a military bearing Johan had seen only in the British Army. A shock of blaze red hair and a mustache that suited him well identified him as most likely an Irishman. The sergeant looked back at him in an appraising matter. Johan smiled knowingly at the man and nodded his head in the acknowledgment of one fighting man to another; he understood what it was like to be assigned an officer that was full of nothing more than piss and wind.

"I don't have times for pleasantries," the Lieutenant was saying. "I am searching for two white captives taken by the savages last month down near the Iowa border."

"You lost their trail." Johan stated the obvious. "And you think I might have seen them."

"There is supposed to be a large camp a day's ride west of here. Have you been there?" the Lieutenant asked as he looked to the horizon.

"There are about fifty lodges there, on the north side of the creek and the lee side of the hills, maybe twenty miles. The chief is named Bald Eagle; a good man, honest and brave."

"Were there any white captives in the village?" The Lieutenant clearly wanted to make his mark, and was impatient for glory. It was the kind of attitude that would get men killed. If he took such a tone with Chief Bald Eagle he would find his scalp decorating a lance.

Johan wondered what this dandy would think if he knew the man standing before him had seen hard campaigning on and off for more than a decade while serving with the toughest fighting force in the French Army and certainly among the toughest in the world. The young pup likely didn't appreciate the difference between a veteran and a cadet. Johan looked hard again at the men behind the Lieutenant. These were men who took soldiering seriously; they seemed experienced and the column had deployed skirmishers and vedettes like men who knew what they were about. Johan looked at the carbine in the hands of the sergeant; it was at half cock with a cap on the nipple, ready for immediate use. It was one of the Sharps he had heard so much about. These men were well armed and competent.

Would these men be a match for the Lakota he had seen? It was an interesting question, but his first thought was no. They were too few and they were not well led. Old Chief Bald Eagle would swallow them up and spit them out. Although, the old chief would know there had been a fight.

Johan looked up at the Lieutenant and ran his hand through his beard as he spoke. "I haven't seen a white woman in eight months. Last one I saw was down by New Ulm last spring. Would any of your men have a pinch of tobacco?"

"Except for your wife, you mean," the Lieutenant said as the Sergeant passed a plug of tobacco to the Lieutenant who passed it down to Johan.

"No, she is a breed." Johan pulled out his pocket knife and shaved a pipe full of tobacco from the plug and returned the tobacco to the Sergeant. Then he turned to look at Mina and switched to French. "Mina, the young pup thinks you're a white woman and my wife!"

Mina smiled at the Lieutenant and replied in French. "Well, I have claimed you, Johan. Otherwise I might have taken a husband of one of Chief Bald Eagle's sons."

Johan laughed, and turned to the Lieutenant. "Mina has me better trained than any white woman would have! Would your men like to camp with us tonight or do you plan to push on towards the next creek? It's been three or four months since our fire has seen either tea or coffee. If you have some, Mina might be convinced to make some bear sign to trade."

The Sergeant got down from his horse and tossed Johan a small bag of coffee. "Ye chose a good spot. Been in the Army?"

The Lieutenant glared at the Sergeant's back and spun his horse away from them as the rest of the command arrived, dismounted and began the preparations needed for a camp. The command had been unspoken, and the Sergeant had given it, not the Lieutenant.

Johan grinned at the Sergeant. "Not this one. I served with the Foreign Legion in the Crimea and Africa."

The Sergeant chuckled. "We've ate some of the same dirt then. I was with that damned fool Cardigan."

Johan appraised the man again. "The Valley of Death?"

The Sergeant shook his head in silent acknowledgment. "Into the valley of death rode the six hundred. I spent the next eight months in hospital."

Johan would have to rethink the chances of the Lakota; one veteran of this caliber could make an enormous difference. "Hand me your cup and your name."

The Sergeant raised an eyebrow and handed Johan his tin cup. "Sergeant Finian Reilly."

Johan reached down, pulled a tuft of dry grass and quickly wiped down the inside of the cup. Then he reached beneath Mina in between two buffalo hides to haul out his last bottle of cognac. He poured the Sergeant a good dose of medicine. "For what ails you, Sergeant Reilly."

The Sergeant took his cup back with a grateful smile. "Thank you."

Johan raised the bottle in a toast. "Sevastopol!" The Sergeant raised his cup and echoed the toast.

Their toast brought the attention of the young officer; he sat his horse now some thirty paces away, a pair of field glasses held half-raised, and looked to them with an envious expression. Fool. "How long?" Johan asked in a lowered voice as he inclined his head towards the young officer when the other had turned away again, raising the field glasses to scan the horizon.

He trusted the Irish veteran to know the meaning of his question. "He left West Point last year. He's hungry for glory and spoiling for a fight. If he lives, he might make a decent enough officer."

Johan smiled. "Your Captain sent you along to make certain he would do nothing stupid."

Sergeant Reilly smiled wryly and raised his cup again in agreement.

Johan felt his face darken as he remembered a particular young officer with illusions of glory. How many had died because of his ambition? Remi had found the boy soldier outside a brothel and slit his throat. It had been justice, but it had been too late.

Johan looked at the Sergeant carefully then pointedly looked down at the knife at his hip. "There are many Lakota in the area…" He purposefully let his words linger.

The sergeant smiled slightly again. "'Tis an idea, but no. He'll grow up. Thank ye kindly fer the offer though." The man looked at Johan with considering eyes. "They be talking of Secession in the South; sure an' if they do, it'll bring a war. We could use men of your stripe."

Johan thought of the words and eyed the carbine hanging from the man's hip. He missed the life of a Legionnaire, but now he had Mina. Rather than answer the unspoken question he looked at the carbine the sergeant held. "What do you think of that Sharps?"

Fort Abercrombie, Dakota Territory, Winter 1861

Being on the frontier, Minnesota saw the Regulars of the US Army stripped from frontier garrisons to fight the Rebellion. Volunteers took their place. At these isolated frontier garrisons, men learned the trade of a soldier before they were sent to war. As the war progressed, men were needed and those garrisons were reduced. Some were eliminated entirely, a practice that would have dire consequences during the "Dakota Uprising" of 1862.

eth lowered his head under the blanket and blew into his hands to warm his fingers, listening to Sebastian's kitten, Mossy, mew softly in the next bunk. He smiled as his hand brushed across his letter to Carlie. Feeling a draft of cold air slip under the blanket, he pulled it tighter around him in a vain effort to stay warm. Even with the wool gloves, drawers, two shirts, a sleeping cap and a scarf, he could not get warm. The blanket the government provided was too thin, so he had bought another heavier blanket and slept rolled up in that as well. Regardless, he had to sleep curled into an uncomfortable ball to even pretend to stay warm. His feet and hands hurt from the cold and he couldn't seem to keep all of him under the blanket. He felt Allen stretch out behind him; he was grateful for the extra heat Allen provided. Sharing a bunk with a friend was not so bad, and in winter there was no need to worry about sharing fleas and lice, as the cold killed them off.

Seth let his mind wander in all manner of directions as he tried to ignore the calling of his bladder. If a man wasn't quick about his business outside he would get frostbitten, and the sinks were a good fifty yards outside the door. As much as he hated to use the thunder jug, he was weighing his options. A good hot steaming cup of coffee two hours before tattoo went a long way toward warming the soul but it also meant being woken up with a full bladder two hours before dawn and holding it for as long as possible.

The two candles in the barracks room gave the place a lurid, half-hearted glow. It may have raised the heat in the room a tiny bit, but he doubted it. He would have preferred a roaring fire to the candles but some damned fool had decided there could be no fire after tattoo; bastard.

Then there was Johan, Sergeant Steele; oh, how Seth would have dearly loved the opportunity to wring his neck! He knew the man from the winter he had worked on the farm, and Seth *had* thought the man liked him. But he was a Sergeant now, with the stripes on his sleeves that gave him authority. Didn't the damned fool know it was too cold outside to do anything more than the bare minimum? And what kind of idiot brought his wife to the army with him? Yes, she was pretty and could cook and sew, but she had no place with men in the army!

It was amusing to watch her scurry from one building to another wrapped in every bit of clothing she owned. She looked like a moving closet!

He winced as he accidentally touched his nose with his hands. The bastard Sergeant Steele didn't have to hit him so hard yesterday. It had been a legitimate question! What was the point of learning bayonet drill? It wasn't like the war would still be going on in the spring, and they could have better used the time gathering more firewood. But instead of listening to the wisdom of his words, the bastard had tossed him that stupid wooden 'fencing' rifle and told him to stay warm by working. The cursed bayonet drill that everyone knew they would never need to use.

Seth knew why he was so disgusted with Sergeant Steele, and it probably wasn't fair. He was so sick of drilling. Drill in the morning, drill in the afternoon, day after day of the same thing. No one quite understood Steele's intent with formation yesterday; forming the whole company and marching them across the parade ground. Then he and Sergeant Webb had walked along behind, tapping men on the shoulder and telling them to sit down and ordering the others to close ranks. They'd done it three or four times, then Sergeant Steele and the officers had talked just out of earshot of the men. Steele's comment to them had simply been, "Now you know what to do when you take casualties." That, more than anything, bothered Seth. He didn't like that the man expected men from the company to be wounded and killed. They'd give the Rebels a volley or two and watch them run away.

Sergeant Steele's language on the parade ground during drill was abhorrent. The curses he threw at the men were sickening, demeaning beyond measure. Seth wished the man understood a sense of civility and reason. There was no need to curse and howl at the men, it was unnecessary! A simple request and a gentle nudge or demonstration would suffice. The language the man used would surely lead him away from the Lord.

Seth took a deep breath and tried to calm his spirit. It wasn't Christian of him to feel such venom towards any man. It was just Steele's cursing bothered him in such a way that he sometimes found himself despising the man. And the proximity of such vile language seeped into his brain. To his everlasting shame, Seth found himself sometimes using such curses himself.

He knew in his heart that Sergeant Steele was merely making every effort to turn them into soldiers. Seth just wished he had the experience and the knowledge to be a Sergeant, to have the ear of the officers and other NCOs who respected that knowledge. It was envy, a sin. He had to stop or it would consume him.

Seth peeked out from under his blanket. There was Bryce swinging in that ridiculous hammock. How he managed to stay warm was a mystery to Seth. Emmanuel and Nate were sleeping in the bunk above him, and every once in a while he could hear Nate mutter to himself in that distinctive childlike voice. Across from him, Sebastian huddled curling his enormous frame around his ridiculous little kitten. He was alone in his bunk with his army issue blanket and that big saddle blanket he had bought from the volunteer Cavalry because Bryce had opted to sleep in that crazy hammock. Above Sebastian, William and Kevin slept blissfully.

Why did Kevin insist on carrying all those knives? He carried at least four and had at least as many more in his kit.

Seth looked back toward Bryce. He wished he could make more progress teaching the man to read. Being literate was so important. He just couldn't grasp a lack of interest to learn how to do so. A book was a friend that never told you he was too busy or too tired. Anything you ever needed to know, you could find the answer in a book.

It was at least another three hours until reveille and he had to use the sinks. He was going to have to get up and go to the privy. Maybe he could last another twenty minutes…? No, it was time to get his trousers and shoes on, plus his extra shirt and coat and great coat. Curse it all. He did not want to deal with the cold, but if he didn't he was going to get wet.

Mina was so cold that she ached all over; she had never even imagined a bone chilling cold like this! And the snow! Good Lord, but she had never even imagined snow such as this. It came down sideways at times, and there was no way to keep it out of her room. It crept under the door and through tiny gaps in the wall.

She thought winter at the Barnaby homestead had prepared her; she was wrong. This place held little that slowed the howling wind. The wind that used to whisper secrets to her now bit at her ears and fingers. It snarled and mocked her, telling her she would have been better off back in bondage, because it was *never* this cold in

Charleston. And the buildings here were not built half so well as those at the Barnaby's. Even with her jacket, coat and every stitch of clothing she owned, the icy chill still penetrated to her very bones. Her fingertips and nose were always numb in this god forsaken place.

Across the river from the fort was a den of thieves such as she had never imagined. The store was meant to rob the soldiers, and she had to shudder at the thought of the saloon. The prostitutes were so uncouth as to make her blush and even the church left a foul taste in her mouth, though she couldn't have said why. The locals called it a town; she called it a hive of villains.

At least here in the fort there were a few other good women, the laundresses like her. Deelia and Marie were both good hard working women. She liked them both for so many reasons. Honest and hard working, both attributes she eagerly credited them with.

Though she did not appreciate the way both would tease her for complaining of the cold. If Mina had a choice she might crawl under those buffalo robes in her bed and never come out except to add a stick to that little pot bellied stove in her room.

Though it wasn't really *her* room, it was the Sergeant's quarters... but of course Sergeant Johan was hers, which meant so was the room.

She liked the way the blue stripes looked on his shoulders and the stripe down his trouser leg was even more striking. He was a soldier and looked far more the part than the wealthy militiamen she had seen in Charleston. His military experience had garnered him a set of stripes and the position of Regimental drill master and Armorer. She knew he had seen real war before; his answer to Seth's question about the Crimea last winter had made that clear.

That meant he held no illusions as to the horror these men would see. Johan thought the war would last several years and probably not change things as much as some hoped. She suspected he was right; though she prayed that he was wrong.

She had to sometimes stop and just watch him. She could certainly hear him; his voice thundered across the parade ground. His distinctive accent had garnered snickers from some at first, but she suspected the men quickly learned to smile to themselves where he could not see them. Mina didn't pretend to understand why they endlessly drilled or marched at the double quick around and around the fort. Though she understood the purpose of Johan teaching them the bayonet, it was a fearsome thing to watch two score men tearing apart the air in front of them. She thought them good students, and Johan a good teacher.

She liked the men of the company; she had taken to calling them her boys. All of them were polite and respectful to her and the other laundresses. None dared speak rudely to them, since there were men here who knew Deelia and Marie, and would come to their defense. And any that thought of speaking ill of her would face the wrath of her Sergeant. The Captain was a good, God-fearing minister which only added to the inherent decency of the company.

She was certain every man in the company had joined the Army out of a need to defend the flag, for something greater than themselves. But like any gathering of men there were bound to be villains in the ranks. Though she admitted she had yet to meet them, at least as far as she knew. She suspected the boy Andy to be a troublemaker, though at the same time hoped that army life under her Sergeant would grow him up.

There were a few abolitionists in the ranks of her boys. Seth, Emmanuel and Nate, to name just a few, and she suspected others like Allen and the big Sergeant Boraas were as well. Others didn't care about abolition and freedom for everyone, they merely wanted a chance at glory and adventure. She had listened and overheard other talk though that convinced her that many did not believe all were created equal.

Mina had little doubt that these men from Minnesota would give good service to the flag. She prayed, though, that Johan would be wrong about how many would fall. His estimate that more than half would not survive the war bothered her like nothing else he had ever said. He had spoken of it like a man who had seen it before, as a man who knew the fate that waited for them when they themselves did not.

That was when he would speak of the Angel of Death. His talk frightened her. And the wistful look in his gray eyes when he spoke of the Angel almost made her jealous. Sometimes she wondered if he had already seen this Angel, and she hadn't yet been ready for him. How could she compete with an ethereal thing like an idea, something of the like she had never heard of or even imagined?

She supposed it wasn't really a bad concept. A beautiful woman who would come to take your soul through the eyes after death was the kind of thing that likely comforted men. But it seemed odd to her; almost sacrilegious.

Of course, Mina didn't pretend to understand men and perhaps this was one of those things she was not supposed to understand. The Angel was a romantic notion that she could appreciate, the kind of thing she might have expected from a Jane Austen novel. Mina expected to see the Lord Jesus when the time came; she knew it in her heart. And that was not romantic notion, but a truth.

She looked down at her battered memory book; she had recreated much of the burned one from memory, and added to it since. It had followed her for better than half her life and was getting near to being full. She was going to have to acquire a new one. But certainly not from across the river! Perhaps she would visit a book store in St. Paul when the regiment returned to Fort Snelling. She caressed the worn leather cover and remembered what it had seen,. She could almost smell the food the recipes contained within could create, and speak again with the people she had met and liked. It was a record of her life; the only evidence she had even existed was contained within the pages bound behind that worn leather cover.

Johan pulled his great coat closer about him and looked at Mina as she slept under the buffalo robe and wool blankets. It was cold. The mercury showed almost sixty degrees below freezing. A man could die in minutes if he was outside on a night like this. He pitied the sentinels. Though they had shelters, it was still dangerously chill for them out in the open air. He placed another chunk of their precious wood in the pot bellied stove and used a smoldering stick to light his pipe. He looked down at his cup, empty of cognac. He had finished his last bottle tonight and he really had no idea where to get another. The traders on the other side of the river were the worst sort of thieves, and only God knew what kind of poison they used to make their whiskey.

Young Barnaby had asked him again if there was to be mail tomorrow. Johan felt himself smile at the thought of that young man shivering over a letter with words written by his pretty little sister, or intently studying his copy of the old Greek Plutarch. To read and write... Mina had tried to teach him. But no matter what she did, they were just scratches on a paper to him. Johan remembered the Barnaby girl, Carlie. She was pretty and had a personality like a butterfly. He could not helped but like her. She had been honest and friendly, a good companion to Mina when there was no one else. Mrs. Barnaby had been nice enough, but she had never been warm towards Mina; Carlie had, and if for no other reason that endeared the girl to him. He had never had a sister... He could only vaguely remember his own parents, and then the work house after they had died. Johan smiled as he remembered Madame Melinda. The grand old Madame had picked him from the work house, and put him to work in her brothel as a boy of all works. Not the kind of upbringing young Barnaby would think appropriate, or even understand.

Johan considered the letter that had been delivered to him before they had left Fort Snelling. It was the first letter Johan could ever remember receiving, and he had to admit he liked the feeling. He took it out and tried again to make sense of the flowing mess of words Mrs. Barnaby had written to him. He just could not transfer the marks on paper into the uttered word; he could not see the connection. Mina had twice read it to him and had composed his reply. The letter was written by Mrs. Barnaby, and in it she explained that Mr. Barnaby had died last fall. Johan felt an odd sense of loss at such news. He really had liked and respected the man. Then she asked him to look after her son Seth.

"Please bring him home safely to us so that we might cherish him as we cherished his father. I ask you to watch over him as you would your own child." When Mina read it to him it sounded formal, like something that an officer would say. It also sounded heartfelt.

At least she had not begged him to send Seth home.

It was an odd feeling, a woman asking him for a real life-changing favor. It had never happened before. Women in the brothel had asked him to pick up things from the market or to deliver notes, but he had never been asked a favor that really meant something. It was an honor, and it felt good. He would do as he had been asked, and he would do his best to see Seth made it home to take over for his father and provide for his family. He was already watching to keep the young man out of the dice games, and had set him on guard duty the one night the company had an opportunity to access the brothel back in St Paul. But could he keep him safe on the battlefield? That was another question. Death had a fickle hand. If she decided a man was ready, there was nothing anyone could do to stay that claim.

Johan wondered about these boys, for most of them were little more than that. The officers by all accounts were good men, and Johan liked all three of them. They were eager, willing to listen and learn.

The older of the two Lieutenants, Kazlowski, was not of Scandinavian descent as about half of the company were. Johan had been surprised when the man had been suggested and then elected a commission, but Kazlowski was well known, intelligent and respected. Allen said his profession was that of a lawyer, but he had given up his practice to join the Army. Though he had not campaigned for on, the commission had been his for the taking.

The Captain was a minister, a man of God; he would have his work cut out for him.

Johan remembered that he had been no older than these boys when he joined the Legion. In fact, he had been younger than most of them. Seth was definitely older than he had been, and his ribald friend Allen Lenquist, who had been made a Corporal on Johan's suggestion. The quiet and watchful William Young and the impressionable Kevin Jaeger who was every bit as good a shot as any man Johan had ever met, were perhaps the same age as he had been when he first donned the Legion uniform. The tough Norwegian sailor Bryce Sieverson and the gentle giant Sebastian Olson, definitely older. Though the pet kitten Sebastian kept was much younger. Sebastian was truly huge with but one man in the regiment anywhere near him in size; Sergeant Boraas.

Then there was the tiny but inexhaustible Emmanuel Lentsch. That one was a puzzle. He could pass as either a man or woman, and his age was impossible to decipher, appearing to be anywhere from twenty to forty years. His *copain* was always the young fresh faced Nate, Nathanial Johnston, who had certainly lied about *his* age. If he were a day over fifteen summers, Johan would have been surprised. But his years - or lack of them - did nothing to conceal his eagerness to prove himself as a soldier. Joshua Svenson was another young one, a schoolmate of Kevin's. Though they were not exactly friends. Still, they worked together well enough. Finally, there was Andy White, a braggart and troublemaker if Johan had ever seen one. His shock of blond hair was bound to be at the heart of any trouble. The Captain called this little group 'Steele's Mess.'

A mess they were, but they were getting better as was the entire regiment. Johan and the other Sergeants had done much to prepare these boys and men for what would face them.

Sergeant Boraas was a good man, and a level headed soldier. Johan thought he had heard it said the man was a teacher by trade. He could believe it, as few would be foolish enough to challenge him and he had a natural air of command about him.

There was also Sergeant Webb. Older than Johan by a dozen years, but he was as fit and ready as any man in the company - or the entire regiment, for that matter.

The lowest ranked Sergeant in the company was Richard Costan. Johan disliked the man from the moment he met him. The man was big and powerful, but a bully who played favorites. A bully was invariably a coward, and not the right sort of man for a Sergeant. Bullies and cowards always got other men killed before they themselves fell.

Johan was the only veteran in the ranks of this company's non-commissioned officers who had been kissed by war. He and all of the other Sergeants had labored long and hard to instill discipline and order into the ranks. They had taught them to march, to form ranks and most importantly how to act as a single cohesive unit. But that said, their discipline left much to be desired. These were not men who would tolerate one of their own being disciplined in the European style, if even the officers thought of it. Johan wasn't certain if that was a good thing or not, though he did have to admit these men had the makings of fine soldiers.

Most of them took poorly to the bayonet, and that surprised him. Few, if any, liked what was his favorite drill, and none seemed to understand that when the time came that they were eye to eye with the enemy they would need to know what he was trying to teach them. When it came down to it, these men would most likely forget their bayonets entirely and use their rifles as clubs. And while a club was useful, it would always fare poorly against a spear.

Though Johan was very pleased at the arms that had been issued to his company, excellent M1841 Rifles which were shorter and a bit handier to use than the rifle he had bought in Charleston. In his opinion they were far superior to anything he had used in the Legion, whether in the Crimea or North Africa. The bayonets issued with these arms were varied. Some were the more familiar triangular style but most were heavy sword bayonets. Johan would have preferred the triangular, as they were lighter, but these were what had been issued. Not that the men appreciated or really understood the difference yet. They were at best enthusiastic amateurs. It was his job to forge them into *useful* amateurs.

He was generally happy with what he saw of the marksmanship of these men. Several were accustomed to hunting, and with the possible exception of Nate all were comfortable with their arms. They would likely hit their marks. Until their targets started shooting back. That was the rub, and it was a rub that Johan had a difficult time making them understand. It was one thing to stand in ranks march and drill until they were sick of it. It would be a wholly different matter when they were under the fire of an enemy battery or skirmishers. Then they would understand that a soldier stands at both ends of the fire as both judge and defendant.

Johan puffed on his pipe and looked again at Mina; she was beautiful when she slept and she was pretty enough when she was awake. There was something intriguing about her neck, and the delicate collar bones below that striking face. The dark eyes and hair and skin the color of caramel never failed to catch his eye, and it had become difficult not to stare at her. It had been a good idea for her to hire on to the army as a laundress. She made good money ,and earned extra on the side cooking for the officers.

The US Army was different than the French in many ways, not the least of which was a lack of camp followers. Johan had always appreciated the whores, laundresses and other sundry women that followed the Legion. They gave good service, in more ways than one. Then there was the lack of a liquor ration. That in particular grated on his nerves. He was used to his cognac... he needed it. And it was hard to come by. Thinking about it, though, the Colonel had a barrel of whiskey in his quarters, and tomorrow the officers were to go into town for a church social. The enlisted men were not invited. Johan smiled at the thought of a whole barrel of whiskey. More than enough for a bit of a liquor ration. Hell, that was more than even he could drink in one night.

He smiled around the pipe stem; there was a smell, a touch, a sound, that always reminded a man of home. Seth said it was a horsehair rug under his feet while reading a book by the stove and the smell of his mother's fresh bread baking in the oven. For Johan, it was the feel of the hair of his woman against his hand while she slept, a pinch of good tobacco in his pipe, and a bit of cognac in his cup. That was as close to peace as he had ever really felt, that was the feel and smell of home for him.

Mississippi, Autumn 1862

In the fall of 1862, the Rebel Generals Price and Van Dorn made an attempt to reverse the flagging Confederate fortunes in the Mississippi River Valley after earlier defeats at Forts Donaldson, Shiloh, and Corinth. At Iuka and a little less than a month later at Corinth, US Generals Grant and Rosecrans badly bloodied the Confederates.

The Confederates lost nearly 12,000 men in the campaign while US losses were less than a quarter of that.

This was the first battle, and the first real introduction to the reality of war for Johan's men. Johan grinned slightly. Today they would learn that war was not a glorious beast. Some men would learn they were not as brave as they thought they were. Strong men would flee and men thought to be mice would stand the fires of hell. While the men had done some hard marching that prepared them physically for the rigors of the march, they had never before marched into the sounds of guns. Many of the regiment had seen death when a deck collapsed on the steamboat they were taking down the Mississippi. But death by drowning, or from being crushed by a collapsing deck, was far different than death on a field of battle. To see and experience cannon actually showering a line of battle with shell and solid shot was a rude and frightening baptism of fire.

For now the regiment, with the rest of the brigade, stood in line of battle waiting for orders. It was a tense time as Rebel guns tried to get their range with shell. It was good that the range was long and that the Rebel gunners were too eager; as a result most of their fire was ineffective. These were not the Russian guns of the Alma or Sevastopol; but they were frightening enough. Johan was glad that no round shot skipped across the field as a minister of death that a man could watch coming for him. Johan could hear Seth uttering a prayer over and over again. He was not terribly familiar with the Bible but he had heard the prayer before, a bit of the Psalms perhaps. "The Lord is my light and my salvation; whom shall I fear?" Johan had to admit that it was oddly comforting.

Johan watched Sebastian reach into his haversack and scratch his cat, and grinned at the absurdity of it of a tiny cat as the pet of such an enormous man. It certainly was not a wise idea to keep the absurd little thing, but it had kept the mice at bay in barracks and several of the men enjoyed the entertainment value of it. Johan was glad he had decided not to make an issue over the kitten. It kept the man happy and was harmless.

Sebastian flinched and ducked away from a spent bullet as it passed over him with a buzz like an angry hornet, then began to inch backward.

Johan aimed a swift kick at the seat of his pants, bellowing, "Keep in line, you monster!" Sebastian hurriedly dressed himself to Bryce.

Sebastian was not the only man who had begun to inch backward. Johan's curses, kicks and swats with the butt of his rifle along with Big Josh's gentle hand upon the shoulder of some men had stiffened the resolve of the company. The unknown was already beginning to tell upon some of the men. The distant boom of cannon and the occasional rattle of musketry was disconcerting to men unused to it.

The Captain let go a prayer in his pulpit voice that Johan did not quite follow. Then spoke: "Steady, men! Only the good Lord can see the courage in your hearts. It's time to put that courage on your sleeves. You stand with your neighbors and with your friends, and you stand here for your families and for your country. Do not let them down!"

Johan grinned as he saw a score of backs stiffen. The Captain knew these men, was the pastor to many. If they ran, he would never forgive them and they knew it.

Johan listened to the crash of musketry ahead and then the thunder of a battery of guns in reply. The noise increased gradually as more men and their regiments were fed into the battle or discovered it on their own. The ordered and calm commands of officers were drowned out by the din of battle.

With a loud howl of pain, Kevin doubled over on the ground holding his shin. A spent bullet finding its mark against him, most likely. A shell exploded over him, and Johan watched a piece of shrapnel the size of his hand rip through the air where a moment earlier Kevin's head had been. The deadly bit of shrapnel tore a furrow in the ground between William and Andy. They both looked at it and then at each other. Andy grinned and had started to say something when another shell exploded high above the company, showering the men with hot shrapnel.

Andy took off his hat to look at a smoldering hole in the brim; then looked down at his trousers and the spreading stain in the front. He was not the only man to have messed himself; both Seth and Sebastian looked sheepish in the knowledge that there was more than just sweat in their trousers. Joshua had been knocked ass over teakettle by a piece of shrapnel the size of a cup. He sat on the ground looking forlornly at his shattered canteen while rubbing a badly bruised shoulder.

Every eye in the company watched a spent solid shot roll to a stop a few score yards in front of the company. Smoke rose from it as it cooled; every eye could see the lethal round ball resting on the ground and all knew that it meant death was all too near.

Johan heard the order to move forward. He bellowed out the order to stay quiet in the ranks unconsciously in French. The line lurched forward. Andy replaced his hat and Kevin and Joshua both stood up to take their place in line. Johan saw the rapidly spreading bloodstain on Kevin's pant leg and Joshua staggering like a drunken fool.

"Jaeger, Svenson, fall out and report to the surgeon. Close up that line!" he shouted. The two men fell out and the line dutifully closed ranks.

Seth was uttering another prayer: "Give thanks in all circumstances; for this is the will of God in Christ Jesus for you." Johan had never heard the words before, but he did not doubt it was from the Bible. Johan almost envied the boy his faith; he was rarely if ever without it.

There was a sudden shrill yell, not unlike coyotes arguing, and a regiment of Rebels erupted from the tree line off to the right charging a battery to its front. Johan cringed in expectation of what the battery was about to do, he could see others in the line turning their heads.

"Eyes front, you damned shit-eating fools! Watch where you're going, not those idiots dying." Johan's command sliced through the din and even though in French the men were familiar enough with his curses to obey his arm gesturing to their front.

A dozen heads swiveled back to the front as six cannon belched forth canister and death into the advancing lines of gray. Entire companies disintegrated and the Angel of Death visited many a brave man.

"Right, half wheel! March!" Johan heard the Captain yell the command and the company obeyed.

"Halt!" The Captain shouted; Johan could feel the tension along the line. The men were tight and nervous.

What was about to happen was obvious to Johan. They were perfectly positioned to pour a flanking fire into the charging Rebels. It would be effective, as long as no Rebel regiment was positioned to do the same to them. Johan looked apprehensively towards the woods three hundred yards ahead of them; skirmishers had disappeared into

111

those trees a few moments earlier and there had been no fire to greet them.

"By company! Ready... Aim!" The wait was agonizing; the Major was giving the men time to pick their targets. One second, another... "FIRE!" The line erupted in flame and Johan instinctively knelt down to look below the smoke. He saw pandemonium among the Rebel ranks. The cannon in front had staggered them and weakened their will, and the single, well-timed volley from an unexpected flank broke them. Gray clad men started to the rear in a trickle and then that trickle turned into a torrent. The regiment broke into a cheer as realization of what they had done spread through their ranks.

"Load!" The Captain screamed though most of the men were already doing so.

Johan looked into those dark trees that skirmishers had disappeared into and worried, he could see the Captain doing the same. Then both saw the muzzle flashes inside the trees, and skirmishers began to emerge from the trees in the dogged fire and move in maneuvers they had been so carefully taught. One of the skirmishers waited too long before moving, and suddenly let out a ragged scream as he was hit. Blood blossoming from his chest, he fell. At nearly three hundred yards, if Johan could see blood fly there was no doubt as to the outcome of such a wound.

He heard the Major give the command but didn't quite believe it. A company right face? That would put the men into a column of fours. "At the double quick!" came the order, and he understood. If the regiment could close the distance and form in time to give the enemy skirmishers a volley, they might gain the protection of the woods themselves.

Johan looked out across the carnage that was called a field of battle and listened. On the other side of the woods he could hear the sounds of guns being hitched to caissons and withdrawn. The steady tramp of marching men was receding instead of coming closer; the battle was over. It would take the Generals time to decide if they would pursue or if the bloodletting had been enough to sate their thirst for glory and laurels. Johan took a short drink from his canteen.

He turned and took the half dozen steps necessary to reach the Captain. The Captain's face was pale. It was easy to see that he was no different than the enlisted men. This had also been his first taste of battle and it affected him no differently. The freshly dead had an effect upon all men, but he had kept his head and done his job. He would do.

"Captain, permission to bring relief to the wounded." Johan asked.

The Captain rubbed a sleeve across his sweaty brow and thought for a moment. "Go ahead, Sergeant, but take only a small detail, and stay within earshot in case the rebels come back."

He nodded and said, "Yes, sir."

Johan slung his rifle as he came up behind his mess. They had done well enough today. No man had run, though a couple had been a touch unsteady. He put a hand on the shoulder of Nate and then Emmanuel. "You two; fall out and come with me. Sling your rifles. We have more work to do." He pointed to the barn fifty yards behind them. "Emmanuel, grab a wheelbarrow or some sacks and bring them back, and a bucket of water if one is handy."

Emmanuel sprinted for the barn and Nate looked up at him with haunted eyes. "Sergeant, is this as bad as a fight will get?" His voice was soft and low, spoken in such a way that it was obvious he did not want his comrades to know he had asked the question.

Johan looked at the powder smeared face, streaked by sweat and fear. Had he ever been that young? "It gets no easier. The first time is hard, the next time a little less so. Eventually you will be numb to it, and it will no longer bother you quite so much. But no, at times it will be much, much worse and pray to God you never come to look forward to it."

Nate took a step back and gestured, "Here comes Emmanuel." Then he whispered, "Thanks."

Johan nodded and turned to see Emmanuel pushing a wheelbarrow with several burlap bags in it. He sighed. It was not so much that he hated what he was about to do, but it was a cold and distasteful thing that he did not like.

He walked to a dead private from B Company, picked up the canteen and tossed it to Nate. Then he pointed Nate toward a clump of a dozen dead Rebels laying twenty yards behind them. "Go get their canteens, unless empty Then leave them."

Nate turned a shade of green and started to protest. Johan shook his head. "They cannot hurt you now. I expect them to be quite peaceful."

Nate obeyed and Johan watched him gingerly pulling the canteens from the dead. He left only one that Johan could see had been shattered by the same round shot which had killed the man. Nate took a step away from the clump of corpses and vomited. Johan turned away to let him be sick without his watching. Emmanuel stared.

"What are the wheel cart and sacks for, Sergeant?" Emmanuel had canted his head slightly to see past Johan's shoulder in order to watch Nate be sick.

"Shoes," Johan said simply.

Nate reached them, his face a bit slick from perspiration and his shoes glistened with the blood he had stood in to retrieve the canteens. He looked green, as though he was about to be sick again.

Johan motioned for the two to follow and they began their errand of mercy. He looked down at a dead Rebel Captain fifty yards in front of the line. "These look to be about the right size for Kevin." He pulled off the boots and tossed them to Emmanuel. Then he quickly and efficiently rifled the dead officer's corpse. He came up with a fat wallet full of Confederate currency and a nice silver watch which he also tossed to Emmanuel. He stood up and said to Nate, "Get his canteen."

The miserable sounds of a man crying for water drew the small detail to another clump of twisted human wreckage. A young man lay there among the dead with a shattered leg. Johan looked him over with the eye of a man who had seen many a field of battle.

"Oh God, please give me some water," the man begged. Perhaps all of nineteen years old, with finely chiseled features. He was going to lose his leg, if not his life.

Johan motioned Nate towards the wounded man. "Give him a canteen. Pray with him if he will let you." It did not matter to Johan that the boy was a rebel. To others it might, but to men who had been on both sides of the fire it was mere decency to help a wounded enemy.

Johan deftly moved among the bodies; stripping shoes, boots and other valuables, depositing them in the sacks. He was careful to leave behind pictures and letters. There were some things that were better left with the dead.

A man screamed in agony and begged for God to let him die. Johan turned and walked towards him. The man had been disemboweled and lay on the ground holding his intestines in his hands. Agony filled his face and voice , and as he saw Johan approached, begged to be killed, for an end the ceaseless pain. Johan hung his head a moment and knelt beside the dying man.

It might take him three days to die. The man's eyes were wide even as he grimaced. "Please. Please end this pain."

Johan pulled his bayonet from its scabbard and nodded that he understood. One quick motion and the man no longer felt anything. Johan wiped the man's lifeblood from the bayonet, and put it away. Nate and Emmanuel both looked at him, neither said a word;

They had heard the pleas of the man for an end to the agony and they understood. But those a hundred yards away in line of battle could not have heard and they stared with undisguised horror and disgust.

"We are done for now. We go back." Johan said quietly.

"You are a cruel, heartless, murdering coward!" Seth watched his words strike Sergeant Steele as though from a blow. His head snapped up and Seth watched the heat rise in the man's face. Seth knew he was about to be slapped to the ground. He braced for the blow but it did not land. The Sergeant's face was as red as an apple and his eyes were the color of a knife blade. Then he smiled, and Seth felt as though he was looking into the face of a wolf and he felt his stomach knot. Good God, if he could imagine the face of the devil that had to be it.

Instead of being struck Seth found himself pinned by the Sergeant's eyes. When he spoke it was with a voice as cold as the grave and it carried to every man in the company. "With a ball in the belly and your guts in your hands you would beg me to end it for you. And I would offer you that same *coup de gras.*"

Seth opened his mouth to say something further, but snapped it shut as he saw the murderous look in Johan's eyes and thought better of it. Sergeant Steele motioned Seth and Sebastian to join him.

"Seth, you take the canteens; Sebastian, the wheel cart." His voice brooked no argument and no one spoke.

Seth started to say something but Sebastian put his hand on his shoulder. "Shut up, Seth." The words were simple and to the point.

Seth and every man in the company had watched the Sergeant murder that poor man. He knew he could never forget it. It was one thing to shoot at the enemy. Trying your best to stop them, but that was battle. What Sergeant Steele had done was nothing short of cold blooded murder.

And then he had come back to the line with a wheelbarrow full of shoes from the dead and a bag full of valuables! The man had robbed the dead! The Captain, Lieutenants and other Sergeants did nothing. Seth couldn't believe it, that wasn't what soldiers were supposed to do, it was thievery and murder! The Captain had just stood behind the rear rank and watched, a single tear working its way down his face. How could he contain his shame? And the Lieutenant! He had just nodded at the returning detail as if nothing wrong had just happened, hadn't he *seen* it? Someone should bring Sergeant Steele up on charges and if the officers and other non commissioned officers wouldn't, then he would! Murder was murder, it wasn't *right.*

The Captain saw Seth looking at him and lowered his head. As he should! The Captain *had* to know he was wrong; he was a minister, for God's sake! He knew the difference between right and wrong!

Seth and the rest of the detail left the line and walked into the carnage strewn battlefield. Seth stepped around a dead horse and into what was left of a man that had been killed by a cannon ball. He was so torn up Seth wasn't even sure if he had been a Confederate or not. The dirt around the man was covered in gore, human mixed with horse; Seth felt his stomach tighten. He had seen slaughtered hogs and cattle before, but never a dead man.

"Get his boots." Sergeant Steele said coldly. The barbarian didn't even have the decency to pray over the man.

Sebastian just stared at the dead man for a moment, then reached down and removed the boots from the body. His face turned a touch green, but he held and didn't throw up. Seth wondered if he would in a similar circumstance. Then a moment later Seth felt his stomach lurch as he watched the corpse come apart. He bent over and vomited for both of them.

"Seth, when you finish get his canteen." Sergeant Steele said brusquely.

Seth could have sworn the man was enjoying himself. Sergeant Steele walked over to a wounded Rebel Corporal. The man was lying beside a shattered tree stump a small framed portrait held in a bloody hand.

"Yanks, some water if you have it to spare. Mine's all played out." The man spoke very calmly as if there was nothing wrong with him.

Sergeant Steele motioned Seth to the man. As he got within a few paces he saw the extent of his injuries. A tourniquet was wrapped tightly around what was left of his right leg. Something had smashed it just above the knee. At least it was no longer bleeding. Seth handed the man a canteen and it was accepted gratefully.

"There will be a stretcher along and they'll take you to the surgeons." Seth said, realizing as he said it that he had seen no one with a stretcher yet.

The Rebel drank long and hard from the canteen and looked up at Seth. His eyes were green, green as fresh clover, but he looked up at Seth with a vacant look and smiled. How could he smile? His leg was gone!

"Y'all played merry hob with us today. We'll lick you next time though." He spoke with a hollow voice as though he spoke from the bottom of a rain barrel.

Seth knelt beside him, not caring about the detail or Sergeant Steele. "What's your name?"

"Brian Swift, I'm from…" The man stopped short and looked off past Seth's shoulder. "Is that an angel?" he asked with a bit of excitement in his voice. "I ain't never seen an angel afore… gawd, she's beautiful!"

Seth turned to look at what the man was talking about. There was nothing there but the line of battle with the flags fluttering. He turned to ask the man what he was talking about and saw his eyes fixed in place, a peaceful look upon his face. Seth just stared at the dead man.

Sergeant Steele spoke from behind the man. "Did you get his name?"

Seth started, then replied; "Brian Swift."

"Good, you always carry a bit of writing paper. Write his name on a bit of it. Put that *cartes de visite* in his pocket," the Sergeant said. "And shut his eyes."

Seth stared at the Sergeant a moment; then did as he was told. His fury and righteous rage were gone, dashed against the reality of war.

Mina looked across the tent that Johan had bought for her so long ago. It really wasn't much, but it kept her dry and gave some privacy. Two people could set the tent in ten minutes or so and she willingly shared it with the other laundresses. They all appreciated the space, and none complained of having four women in an area many would say was good enough for only one.

The men appreciated the laundresses - her in particular. Johan even went so far as to accuse some of loving her. They praised her cooking, her sewing, and even occasionally called her beautiful. In Mina's opinion, young Elissa was the pretty one. She had always thought of herself as rather plain and the other ladies would fall into that same category.

She and Deelia had been the only women willing to set foot in the hospital, a filthy and grotesque place. Tables were set chest high, and the surgeons and their assistants usually stood bespattered with blood as they cut and sawed off shattered limbs. Johan called the surgeons the angels of death, and she understood why. But unlike *the* Angel of Death, there was no wishful yearning to his manner or words, and she understood that too. But those men who survived still needed tending. Johan called her mother and sister to all of the regiment; she was their goddess. Mina scoffed at such talk... but she had to admit she liked it.

And the men showed their appreciation of their efforts. A dying lieutenant had willed her his camp desk, a tidy little bundle made of thin wooden slats tucked into leather pockets that unrolled to expose a good writing surface. She had made good use of it after his death. Many a soldier's family received a letter from their loved one written in her hand.

For far too many it had been the last.

A sergeant of a Wisconsin Regiment who was all but delirious from the ravages of a belly wound had begged her to help him die. Instead, she had sat beside him holding his hand and praying for his immortal soul during the last hours of his life. The letter she had written his family had elicited a response of heartfelt thanks that brought tears to her eyes whenever she thought of it.

In fact, the only letters she had received in her time with Johan had been from grateful families thanking her for her humanity. Every one of those letters touched her heart, and she shared them with Johan. He and others had occasionally taken to calling her the 'Angel of the Regiment.' She appreciated the title all the more because she knew the men meant it.

Many a nurse and laundress received letters from the families of soldiers. Some were in thanks for their woman's touch while others were more earthy, containing dire warnings to stay away from their boys! Oh, the humor in such a warning! These men were not pretty in the field. Sweaty, smelly and filthy; she and all of the laundresses had seen man at his least romantic. And done the laundry to boot!

Mina knew there were men who had romantic notions about Elissa, Deelia and Emaline. Only Deelia was mature enough to really face such an emotion. Emaline and Elissa both had suitors but between Deelia, Marie and herself, she doubted either of the young women likely to find themselves in trouble any time soon. Though, she had to admit that Emaline was often more trouble than she was worth.

When Emaline worked she worked well, but getting her to work was often a problematic issue at best. The girl liked to write letters to anyone she thought would reply, and Mina suspected some of those letters were thoroughly inappropriate. She had to be the center of attention, Emaline did, and when she wasn't she made every effort to become so. It was annoying, and sometimes outright angering. Mina had spoken with her about it, as had both Deelia and Marie, but their words failed to have any impact. Mina had to keep reminding herself that when she was willing to work, Emaline did work hard. She was another set of much-needed hands, and could not be casually sent away.

Maybe... maybe she was competing with Elissa? Though both caught their share of men's eyes, of the two, Elissa was the younger and prettier. She was the quieter and more composed of the two as well. She would make one of these boys a good wife, one day. Mina had little doubt that one of the soldiers would ask for her hand, and no doubt that one would be accepted. She was such a hard worker and rarely complained... No, that wasn't quite true. Elissa didn't complain because plaints changed nothing. Instead, she raged. Her rage was something to behold.

Mina took a moment and thought of what she had seen with the army. A brutal winter at Fort Abercrombie and then a horrible trip to Saint Paul in the spring, battling through snow drifts twenty and thirty feet deep the whole way. After that, the trip south on board a steamboat that had a deck collapse! Men dying before they even reached the battlefield. Then disease had swept the camps, laying low better than half the regiment. Otherwise healthy men struck down by dysentery and typhus, then wasting away in front of her. So many that she feared the regiment would cease to exist before a Rebel was even seen.

Finally they had found the war at Iuka and Corinth; men died by the score and were wounded by the thousands. Was it worth it, this fighting over towns few if any of them had ever even heard of?

At first she had listened to the fighting from the camp, foolishly hiding in her tent with the other laundresses. Then the wounded had begun to stream past the camp towards the hospital. Scenes of such horror she could never even have imagined.

First Marie and Deelia, then the rest of the laundress from the regiment, had offered their services at the hospital. The Steward had gladly accepted them, as had the Regimental Surgeon; though at first Major Wellman had tried to turn them back. Mina would never forget the look of shocked realization upon his face when he saw the scores of wounded descending upon his little hospital. He'd looked from the injured to Marie and her bucket of well water, then to the other women who waited patiently behind her and had changed his mind right there. Every laundress from the regiment - and she suspected from the whole brigade - had come to the hospital and helped in some way. Some, like Mina, had helped write letters. Others had cleaned, mopped fevered brows, or helped with bandages. All gave their time and a gentleness that the wounded men appreciated.

Vicksburg Campaign, 1863

The Vicksburg campaign was arguably the most decisive of the war, effectively splitting the Confederacy in half. The Confederacy never recovered from the simultaneous losses at Vicksburg and Gettysburg. The Vicksburg campaign was perhaps the beginning of the end for the Confederacy.

The whole regiment was covered in dust, sand and sweat, and the smell that emanated from them had to have been overpowering. Sweat and filth were not pleasant scents. Johan knew the odor was there, but he had gotten used to it, and thus could not be bothered by it.

Perhaps a third of the men in the regiment were sorely in need of new shoes, but not a man in Johan's mess and only a couple in the company needed footwear. He had been careful to make certain that every man in his charge started the march with a spare set of shoes. He had also cultivated a cobbler, Corporal Glenn in Sergeant Webb's mess, helping to make certain the man earned a set of corporal stripes in exchange for his services. Though Glenn was a good man, and likely would have done the job even without the stripes.

Johan sat down to rest with the rest of the regiment. Ten miles in two hours while deep in enemy territory. It was a task that he would never have considered while in the Legion. They had only hard crackers and some salt pork for their rations and they expected to meet the enemy at any moment. The skirmishers were out and the brigade was ready for battle.

These men were no longer green. Iuka and Corinth had hardened them and long marches on short rations had only furthered that hardening. Johan looked around. Nate and Emmanuel were sitting back to back, using each other as pillows and Seth was sleeping on his blanket roll with Allen using his legs as a pillow. With the exception of Bryce and Andy, the entire mess was laying down with their feet to the road, taking full advantage of the short rest they had been given. Already this army had vanquished the rebels at unheard-of names such as Forty Hills and Raymond, where a score of men fell from the sun instead of rebel bullets. At Jackson the regiment had formed in support of an Iowa Regiment which had suffered greatly. All were victories with only slight injury to his company. Now they were on the move again, and the pace was as tough as any Johan had ever maintained. He took a moment to sip from his canteen and think longingly of the bottle of cognac secreted in his bedroll.

It was their turn; today if there was a battle, these men would see the firestorm. Would they be as steady as they had been at Iuka and Corinth? Johan hoped so. Their steadiness might make the difference between victory and defeat or life and death.

The distant thunder of cannon stirred them. The lead division must have found Pemberton. Of his mess, only Kevin and William raised their heads to look towards the rising crescendo of cannon. The rest of the men were too tired to care.

A battery of guns charged by on the road at a full gallop, then a regiment of Iowa men at a quick pace. They kicked up enough dust to coat the men of resting regiment in a fine layer, adding yet another coating of grime to their already filthy visages.

The order was passed down the road: "Regiment; fall in!"

Johan rose, looking to his right and saw the other sergeants tiredly taking their places. The corporals followed, and finally the men wearily moved into place.

"Forward, march!" The order passed down the column and the men began to move at their ground-eating pace.

The brigade moved forward and took up a position of reserve. From there regiments would be fed into the battle where they were needed most. A staff ass - as the men called any staff officer - rode up to the Lieutenant Colonel and ordered the regiment to the support of a battery of Logan's Division. Johan heard the order. "At the double quick; forward march!"

The regiment moved forward through an interval in Logan's line and took up position in support of the battery. The acrid smell of powder wafted through the ranks as the cannon continued to belch fire and steel into the enemy. Johan absently ran his thumb along the smooth wood of his rifle stock. It was comforting and the weight of the weapon reassured him against the familiar gnawing twist in his stomach. Johan was not such a fool as to say he felt no fear, and it gnawed at him now. This place was hot and the enemy was in desperate straits. If they lost the battle here, then so too would be the war, and if it was that obvious to him it would be equally so to the Rebels.

The Rebels saw the movement of the regiment to support the battery, and directed a battery of guns upon them with shell. Thankfully, their fire was high. Johan looked to what he could see; the Rebels were beaten and withdrawing from the field, some all but in a rout. He let out a sigh of relief. He had been wrong. The regiment and his mess would be spared again.

"I'll shoot the first man that discharges his weapon!" Johan heard the order and turned his head, for a moment confused. Then he saw that two companies had been wheeled to face a Rebel company. A Rebel Captain and a score of his men were advancing with their arms above their heads; surrender was preferable to death for these men. They were not cowards. There was no doubt of that. But with a section of guns to their front and an entire regiment on their flank, surrender or annihilation were their only options.

Johan took a moment to wipe the sweat from his forehead, and felt his jaw drop in surprise as hundreds of Rebel soldiers streamed by a few hundred yards in front of them. A quick push and the regiment could capture hundreds, perhaps thousands. Yet the Colonel did nothing. Was the fool blind? Then the battery to their right opened with shot and shell into the milling enemy. The destruction was apparent immediately. Scores of men fell, and Johan could hear the screams even over the thunder of the guns.

Then a regiment volleyed into them and more men fell; they ran and tried to escape, but scores were beyond hope. Johan shook his head in despair. The wise officer had surrendered. The fool had gotten his men killed for nothing; there was nowhere they could have gone with the battery and enemy on two flanks. Surrender or die, and they had chosen to die. How many good men had just perished or been wounded for nothing?

It was but a few days since the decisive victory at Champion Hills; the Rebs were crushed there. Unfortunately, no one had bothered to tell the Vicksburg garrison that. Johan felt his stomach knot as he stumbled over the body of a dead man. His automatic glance toward the man's shoes showed that death had been neither quick nor painless. He didn't have time to grab the footgear. Not that it would have mattered, as only Sergeant Boraas had such huge feet. He pushed himself forward again at a dead run into the hail of lead from the enemy works. If he could get into the ditch with the rest of the skirmishers, he might survive this fight.

Almost as soon as the thought crossed his mind he felt the concussion from a shell as it detonated over his head and he found himself looking at the sky with his rifle uncomfortably wedged underneath him. *Merde*, but it was hot. Johan ran his hand across his body… he was intact.

He rolled onto his belly and got to his feet. He could see the ditch where the men, his men, tried to avoid the hellish enemy fire. He closed his eyes and sprinted for the ditch. He felt a tug at his coat and fell onto his face; a score of bullets passed close over him like a pack of angry hornets, killing the space he had occupied only a moment before. He crawled forward the last few yards and rolled into the dubious safety of the ditch.

When he opened his eyes he was staring into Andy's empty gaze. The young man looked surprised, his mouth open as though about to curse. The life had been dragged out of him along with his brains; dragged from his skull by a Rebel bullet. Johan rolled deeper into the ditch.

Allen clapped him on the back. "Thought you were dead, Sergeant; glad I was wrong."

Johan looked at the man and smiled. "Captain told me to take a couple men back to the surgeon. Angel of death told me to get on the table; I told him to bugger off. We still alive?"

Allen laughed. "Andy is done for, Seth is wounded. I think Kevin is a bit mad 'cause he keeps trying to charge the Rebs all by his lonesome. Sebastian is down in the bottom of the ditch crying like a babe; Reb bullet killed his cat. Lieutenant Sanderson and Sergeant Costan are dead, Corporal Kossak is out of his wits bleeding from his head enough for us all."

Allen ducked away from a pair of bullets that smashed into the side of the ditch a few inches from his head. "BULLOCKS! This is insane!"

Johan laughed at the quick shift. "It could be worse."

Allen took a swallow from his canteen. "You stupid Dutchman. How in the hell could it be worse?"

"They could have mortars." Johan leaned back against the side of the ditch and closed his eyes in relief. The pain in his leg irritated him. He looked down at the bloody bandage wrapped around his thigh. Damn it all, those pants had been a good pair, he'd liked the reinforced britches. It had taken real work to steal those off that cavalry laundry line and he wasn't likely to find another undefended laundry line for some time.

Johan listened to the cannon roar and thousands of muskets firing. Men were dying as he lay there but he was alive. He looked down the ditch and saw the Captain and a pair of privates huddled in the bottom of the ditch over the body of the Fourth Sergeant. The Captain was praying, perhaps giving the Last Rites. Joshua, Emmanuel and Nate were passing rifles to Kevin and William, who were doing their best to keep Rebel heads down. From the volume of fire it was inviting in response, they were irritating someone.

Johan motioned to Allen. "Go tell those two to move twenty paces further down the ditch; they'll have a better field of fire and more protection. Give me your rifle."

Allen handed over the weapon. "Good luck, she's loaded."

Johan chanced a glance and saw the Rebels draw back a gun from an embrasure to reload it and a man step forward with a rifle to take aim. He brought up his rifle and shot the man, dropping back into the ditch cursing. The movement hurt his leg. Though not half so much as the dozen bullets smacking into the dirt where he had been a moment before would have.

Johan lay below the lip of the ditch and took in a deep breath; the acrid smell of powder mixed with the thick pungent smell of blood and spent bowels filled his senses.

He took a look down the line; William and Kevin had moved where he had suggested. There was just enough of a curve in the ditch there to shelter them from the fire of the enemy and offer them a decent field of fire down the length of the enemy works. Johan slid further to the left and risked a quick glance at the works.

Two bullets smacked into the ground in front of him, splashing dirt into his face. That might just prove to be rather unhealthy if he tried it again. He slid down to the bottom of the ditch and reloaded his rifle. He left it there and popped up just long enough to send a round through the embrasure with Allen's weapon. He doubted he hit anything, but it was bound to make someone nervous.

He looked up to see Allen moving toward him crouched almost in half as he moved; he was well below the lip of the ditch. "Give me back my rifle, Sergeant."

Johan shifted a little further to the left; he had a good view of a corner of that embrasure from where he was at. The Rebels likely would have to expose themselves to shoot at him. He shifted a little further to the left and heard a howl from below him.

"Hey! You're standing on my head! Move!" Johan moved. Bryce had dug himself a hollow well into the side of the ditch and was almost buried. He no longer had the M1841 Johan liked so much but a big seventy-one caliber French musket of the same model Johan had carried in the Crimea.

"Where the hell did you find that?" Johan asked in surprise.

"On the way to the ditch, a Reb ball smashed my barrel; bruised my arm something fierce. This was just sitting there in the dirt and I figured it was as good as any." A piece of grapeshot tore a chunk of the ditch away above

Johan's head. "Damn it, Sergeant! Would you move, you're attracting fire!" Bryce started to dig deeper into the side of the ditch.

Johan shook his head and moved back towards Allen. The young corporal stood up just enough to clear the lip of the ditch and took quick aim to send a bullet through the embrasure. Before he could fire, and as Johan yelled at him to get back down, a bullet took off the side of his head. Johan rushed to the crumpled form knowing it was pointless. The man was dead.

Johan lay back against the side of the ditch and sighed. If they could hold on till nightfall they could withdraw under the safety of darkness... too many men could die before then. In the course of eighteen days, the men had marched most of two hundred miles and won five victories; four of them in six days. The Rebs had suffered better than five thousand casualties and lost most of ninety guns. All on five days of rations without tentage and with very little rest. But Johan had a feeling that meant nothing; this city would take a siege... another Sevastopol.

It was the 22nd of May, eight years and a few weeks since he had cheated death in front of Sevastopol. He looked down the ditch to the men still trying to keep things hot for the Rebs and then looked at Bryce in his hole. He tossed Allen's brain-spattered rifle to Bryce. "Here; better than that big seventy one."

Johan rubbed the scar on his neck and smiled. The beautiful lady that was the Angel of Death had not come for him yet today. She was not a considerate or fair woman; she came for you when she was ready and she waited for no man. The only solace when facing her was her beauty.

Brother,

I am pleased to have received your letter; to know you are well and only injured in a minor way. Of that I am heartfully glad. The papers say the most terrible things of our fortunes in the war as of yet; your letters revealing the truth of matters are most welcome and I make a point to show them to the men who are too old and too young to serve their country. The wasteabouts who are too cowardly or have decided that they are too important to serve the Union, I shun. Cousin Celia snubbed the banker's son. I'm certain you remember him, as he was the first to call for the crushing of the Rebellion but was noticeably absent when it came time to join the call to arms.

You must tell us more stories of Sergeant Steele and his antics, as they amuse us immensely. Is it true that all of the families of the South own slaves? I doubt it can be so, but Aunt Rosemary insists that it is.

As you know, we are hard set at home to make all of the bills since father died. The monies that we receive from you are a gift as if from God. Your cousins have all left for the War in the last month and their wives and daughters have come from the city to our home in the country. They have helped much with the work about the farm. One of the oxen stepped into a gopher hole and broke a leg; we had no choice but to butcher it. I think I can say without boasting that cousin Celia and I did a good job of it ourselves. The butcher has joined the cavalry and his wife is a poor substitute so we did took up the task. Alicia and Sarah are quite helpful about the farm. Young Alicia has more enthusiasm than sense around the stock, but she makes every effort to earn her keep. Sarah has been sewing and knitting nearly the day long. She insists that we sell her labor to the drygoods store so that she may earn her keep. It is a pity that her husband died of the fever at Island Number Ten, she mourns constantly. But she is making do for her children; I have told her she and her boys can stay as long as she wishes. The children take great joy in feeding the cattle and helping about the farm. They are too young to understand that they will not again see their father.

However, Aunt Rosemary is another matter entirely. She is not suitably attired for the farm and all but refuses to do anything but act ladylike. She insists on wearing hoops around the house and believes the latest New York fashion must be worn in the country; the mud and manure have done a splendid job of conspiring against her. She refuses to help in the kitchen, as she believes such work is beneath her and wishes to know why mother has no maid! Mother and she have twice had terrible rows, and I believe she will drive mother mad before the month ends.

On Saturdays we sit about the stove rolling bandages and knitting socks. We do what we can for the cause and the men in the field who are suffering so; but I fear that working the farm and attempting to keep it from the debtors has prevented us from doing all that we might like.

Mother and I depend upon the monies you send to us. Despite this, we unanimously entreat you to do your duty. Do not shirk danger on our account! I know some of the local Copperheads have been writing poisoned letters to the men who are braver than they; trust that letters you receive from me are true and question the honesty of any that bring sad tidings. Your family is healthy and loves you for your sacrifice.

I shall close this short letter with hope and a prayer. God bless you and keep you safe.

Your Sister Carlie

Johan smiled around his pipe as Seth set down the letter. "You have a good family, Seth. Good people. You have no idea how gifted I was to be able to work for your father that winter. I do envy you your family."

Seth blushed slightly. "Thank you Sergeant. What about your family, surely you have someone other than Mrs. Mina?"

"No, I have no one," Johan said around his pipe stem. "They are all dead."

"I'm sorry."

Johan laughed. "Why? I barely even remember them. As far as I know, my parents died of fever when I was a child."

"Who raised you?" Seth rubbed his bandaged arm absently as he fed a couple sticks into the fire.

"I grew up in a brothel." he said nonchalantly as he knocked the ash from his pipe.

Both Seth and Sebastian stared in surprise. "A whore-house…"

Johan laughed again. "The Madame of the house picked me up from the poor house and used me as a boy of all works. I was thankful for the improvement in food and quarters."

Sebastian laughed heartily, "I'll just bet you thought it an improvement. Better food, and I'll wager better scenery."

Johan shook his head at Sebastian. Seth thought the man simple and innocent for his keeping pet cat, and his tears over the loss of the creature had only reinforced the idea. But Johan knew Sebastian was far less naïve than Seth believed. "Most were not much to look at. Before you ask it, no, I never sampled the wares. I ran errands, emptied the slops and thunder jugs along with a host of other humble chores. Nothing sordid like your young mind imagines."

"But you saw them… naked." Sebastian fairly glowed at the thought.

Johan poured a touch of whiskey into his cup and scoffed at the idea. "A prostitute will kill you quick as a kiss. Anyone who tells different has never seen them work. A man dies in their bed; I make the body disappear. If he got too rough she might put a stiletto between his ribs; I make the body disappear. He hurts a girl; the madam pays a man to slit his throat and I make the body disappear."

"Sweet God... you jest." Seth said looking at Johan as though for the first time.

"No, I am quite serious. I have seen so much 'sin' that I am numb to it. I have killed so often that I no longer really feel regret..." Johan paused a moment and considered. "No, that is not right; God has gifted me with Mina and I feel again. I never thought I might appreciate a woman. I never have. The women I have known were whores; some by circumstance and some by choice. Of them all I only ever considered one a friend. Any one of them would have slit my throat for the contents of my pockets."

"Not all women are like that!" Seth protested angrily.

"You are right... your sister is a good woman, as is your mother, and Mina has opened my eyes to things I never looked to. Yet I wonder if women like your sister and Mina are not exceptions instead of the rule. Have these Rebel women made you think otherwise?"

Seth shook his head. "We are an invading army! If there was no war things would be different. How can I compare the women here to my sister or mother? It isn't a fair measure."

"Do you remember the plantation we passed a couple days back? I listened to Mina speaking to some of the house servants. The master and boy went off to war and left the place in the charge of the women. Forty house slaves and most of two hundred field hands... I cannot imagine such.

The servant called those women far harsher than the men had ever been. " He shook his head in wonder and drained the whiskey from his cup.

"What happened to your friend?" Sebastian asked; he had latched onto the comment of the only whore he had ever considered friend.

Johan looked into his cup and considered the question. How to explain that horrible moment on that parade ground when he discovered he had killed Kyrie's husband; how to describe the moment that had destroyed both of their lives? "I killed her husband," he said quietly.

Seth and Sebastian looked at him, questions on the tip of their tongues.

"Let us talk about you boys and your homes." Johan said as he felt his fist clench involuntarily. He had not told them in so many words to change the subject, he had no need to. He violently shook his head to clear the sudden stab of pain and regret that came with the reality of his remembered youth.

Mina walked up to the fire with young Sven in tow. Her presence brought every man there to his feet and thankfully changed the subject of conversation. She smiled in recognition of the compliment. The firelight made her face glow and the shadows only accentuated her beauty. Seth would say she was doing the work of the Lord here; Johan was never quite sure what to believe, but if there was a God then Mina was surely one of his angels. Her soup and poultices had saved many a life in the regiment and when she visited the hospital there was no doubt what angel was visiting those men. An Angel of Mercy was a welcome change from the Angel of Death; though no less beautiful in her own way.

Sven was not out of place beside her. The boy was perhaps twelve years old and as black as pitch. He had joined them on the Louisiana side as they began the campaign against the city and had stayed with them since. When Sven had come into the camp he had called himself Seven, as it was the only thing the overseer had ever called him. The men had changed his name to Sven and given him cast off bits of uniform. He was a sight but he had a better wardrobe than many a man in the army.

The young man carried his weight within the company and had gained a very real respect from the men. He went everywhere with Mina and did anything she asked of him, though not always without complaint. He fetched wood and water, helped clean pots and pans and generally made himself useful to Mina and the men. In return the company fed and clothed him and even pooled together to pass him most of twenty dollars every pay call. Many had come to see Sven as a tangible symbol of why they were fighting.

"You boys enjoy the mail?" Mina had a voice that was soft and welcome; a touch of home for most of them.

Johan nodded toward Nate. "Nate got himself a nasty letter from a Copperhead lawyer. Coward was trying to convince Nate to desert. He tossed the letter in the fire but keeps asking me if he can talk with you." Johan grinned. "If he proposes I will have to whip him."

Mina laughed and was joined by the others around the fire. "I will have you know, Mr. Steele, that it took me too long to house train you for me to think of a replacement."

Grins emerged on every face around the fire. Even Seth, who had been quite despondent over the loss of his friend Allen, smiled. The thought of their losses made Johan's smile slip. He hadn't expected Seth to help with the burial of Andy, but the dance on the man's grave had been a bit

139

much. Johan knew the two had disliked each other since Andy had made the ill-timed boast that he knew Carlie in the biblical sense. There had been real danger of Seth trying to kill the man, and so Johan had made certain Seth was never behind Andy in the firing line.

Johan turned his head to look toward the supply wagons and their cursing drivers rolling into camp. There had been a steady stream of them all day and well into the night, bringing much needed rations and supplies. He wondered if the mules in the corrals would be as vocal tonight as last; they had kept the camp awake with their loud conversations. The Army mules kept the army supplied, and those in the corral were not about to let anyone forget it.

He lit his pipe again with a twig from the fire and listened to the banter of his men. Kevin was teasing Joshua about something. He would have to talk to Kevin about that; Joshua was always the butt of jokes, and it might easily go too far one day. William and Seth were discussing Shakespeare's comedies...

Johan preferred the tragedies, as they seemed closer to life. Bryce and Sebastian were talking about ships again. Bryce should have joined the Navy; but Johan would be damned if he was not glad to have him on the line.

"Bryce, you ever fire any of those big guns on ship?" He watched Mina disappear towards her tent with Nate and Emmanuel in tow as he asked the question. He cocked his head to the side and wondered what Nate so desperately needed to talk with his wife about. Still, he trusted Mina; if he needed to know, she would tell him.

"I was never on ship with anything bigger than twelve pounders. We never needed to use them for real." Bryce said as he scratched his bearded chin.

"Why not join the navy?" Johan asked absently.

Bryce chuckled. "Those turtles are furnaces. I'd rather be in the Infantry... smells better!"

Every man around the fire laughed at the impossibility of that.

Nothing could smell worse than the infantry.

Vicksburg Provost Guard

Vicksburg was a prize that needed to be defended, and its garrison reflected that. The Provost Guard was the only law in the city and it was not always all that effective. Men often did not deal with the Provost at all, instead choosing to deal with matters in a less formal and sometimes more final way.

ohan scratched the scar under his beard and looked at the surgeon. Thin and blond, with the strong clean cut features that women probably thought handsome, he carried himself like a gentleman, radiated an air of superiority and balked at any kind of menial labor. Johan did not like Major Wellman; he was too proud of himself. He certainly did not like the way the man looked at Mina. Major or not, if he ever tried anything untoward none would find the body.

"Sergeant, bring your detail." The major threw his cigar into a mud puddle; it was only half smoked and now wasted, but that didn't stop Johan from snatching it up. Hopefully he could dry it out enough to transfer some of the tobacco into his pipe.

Johan almost snarled as he ordered his mess to fall in and marched them along behind the surgeon. He was not half the man of the regimental surgeon, Captain Bjornson, and even less of a doctor. Johan considered that the officer could not care less whether any soldier that lay upon his table lived or died. He was in the army for the pay and the prestige that came with the rank of Major.

One man spat on the street in front of the detail. and a woman raised her voice for all to overhear as she whined about the kind of visitors that the war had brought to her fine town. Johan only smiled. It had been a fine town before the war, yes, but the siege had spared few buildings. The richer they looked, the more inviting target they had made of themselves for the artillerists. He had been all about this town and had come to the conclusion that there were as many Union families in the city as Secesch, though they might easily have been fair weather Unionists.

Johan ordered the detail to halt as the surgeon pointed to a large, well-kept house that had been spared the worst of the bombardments. The major started up the stairs. Johan posted Bryce and Sebastian as guards.

And stopped in stunned silence as he recognized the white haired woman standing in the door.

Though to his eyes she was still hauntingly beautiful, there had been changes in the time since he had seen her last. Brilliant white hair had faded slightly, her face no longer held a look of childhood innocence, and faint crow's feet now framed her eyes.

Those were every bit as blue as he remembered. The only change there was the lack of hatred. Perhaps hidden, not likely forgotten, but if she was here then she had done well enough for herself to make it across the Atlantic and set herself in this nice house. She looked well kept; her dress appeared to be of the latest Parisian fashion.

And he would not have expected less. She looked every bit the lady - as she always had.

"Sergeant? You alright? You look like you've seen a ghost," Emmanuel commented.

"I have. A ghost of a life, long past," Johan replied quietly.

Major Wellman was arguing with Kyrie about something and had pulled a small placard from his valise. He waved it in front of her and began to use language that was quite inappropriate in front of a lady. Johan tapped Seth on the shoulder and the pair of them started up the stairs to stop what was about to boil over into an ugly shouting match. He moved as much to stop Kyrie from knifing the major; he was willing to wager she still concealed that vicious stiletto between her shoulder blades, and he could see at least two rather lethal hair pins.

Kyrie saw Johan on the stairs and stared in a moment in surprised recognition. Then she pushed past the surgeon to confront him.

"Sergent, would you tell this protestant swine I will not bribe him! I threw this son of an Englishman from the house on Friday and he returns on Sunday morn threatening to quarantine my house if I don't let him in for free in the future." Her voice was melodious, a pleasure to the ear, though her Dutch was harsh. There was no way the surgeon understood her words

Johan put up his hand to calm her and replied in the language of his childhood, "Madame, what are you saying?"

"This ugly bastard is too cheap to pay for one of my girls and wants me to let him in for free or he will quarantine my house!"

Johan paused for few moments. So she had become a madam like the Lady Melinda of their childhood years. This fine house was a brothel... and he was too jaded to be shocked by anything. "I see. Madame, I will take care of this for you." He considered a moment. "Anything I can do... anything you need is yours." He bowed formally to Kyrie and switched to English for the benefit of the surgeon. "Major, the lady refuses to pay the bribe you demand. If you persist in this I will make a report to the Captain."

The surgeon stared at Johan for a moment in amazement then snarled, "It will be my word against yours, Sergeant."

"I know that, sir. I will be certain to also present letters of introduction from every officer that has ever visited this place."

The surgeon considered a moment. "You had better hope you never cross my table."

"That is a given, sir," Johan said stiffly.

The major looked hard at him, then looked to Kyrie and back again. He then spun on his heel. "Come along, Sergeant. I am needed at the hospital."

"Of course... sir." Johan eyed the man with contempt. He nodded to Kyrie and gathered his men for the march back to the camp.

As they started down the street Seth looked over his shoulder back at the house. "Is that a... a whore house, Sergeant?"

Johan snorted and spat into the street. "Yes. And do not be quick to judge. Those women are trying to survive. They need not beg for a roof over their head or the food they eat. Stay away from there. Your sister would not approve. But I will tell you that many a soldier knows only the embrace of a soiled dove."

"But Sergeant, they are sinful women," Seth protested.

Johan shook his head slightly. "Seth, you know the Bible better than I ever will. Did Jesus not let a whore clean his feet with her tears? If he forgave such a woman, who are we to judge?"

"That's in Luke. You're right." Seth hung his head a moment. He added defensively, "Your judgments are quick and not always very nice."

Johan looked at Seth as they marched down the street; the silence was interrupted only by the tread of marching feet. "Have I ever called myself a Christian? I have listened to your Bible read many a time, and it holds much wisdom and much promise, but it was not meant for a man such as me."

"So what do you believe in, Sergeant?" Emmanuel asked from behind him.

Johan looked at the surgeon. "I know the *real* Angel of Death watches us all, and when she comes calling there is no ignoring her. When she comes for each of us in turn God will judge as he sees fit. I have seen too much death not to know that death spares no man. If I make a few people better off, mayhaps God will look past some of my evil."

Johan had no idea why he spoke so to Seth and the other men of his mess, especially with the Major present. Perhaps it was the shock of seeing Kyrie here.

Long ago she had been his best friend; they had been pulled from the workhouse together, entering the madam's house. While Johan had run away after a fight with sailors and become a soldier, Kyrie had been trained and taught the ways of a lady. The madam had intended to train her up as a whore from the start, but Kyrie was too sharp for that to be the end for her. She had embraced the education in ladylike ways, using that and her beauty as a weapon against the world. She had gained a man of the gentry as a husband... the damned fool who Johan had gutted on the parade ground so many years ago. Now, here she was making a life for herself. He wished her the best. That was all he could really do.

Meantime Seth had brightened. "All you need do is give your heart to Jesus..."

Johan disliked the disruption of his thoughts and interrupted Seth before he could go further. "If he wants my heart all he need do is take it."

Major Wellman interrupted with a rude laugh. "My, my! Isn't your Sergeant the philosophical one? He speaks so to assuage his own guilt for having visited such a place too often. Those women are women of sin, and as such have no hope of redemption. Did you get your wife from a house such as that?"

Johan felt his face color as his left hand dropped to his bayonet.

Kevin saw his reaction and put a hand out to stop him. "He ain't worth it, Sergeant. He's just an officer."

"Not much of one!" Emmanuel snarled.

"So pathetic as to have to pay. Oh great lover, you must show us your ways," Nate added loudly in his best approximation of a woman's voice.

The entire detail laughed at the innuendo. The laughter of his men loosened the rage that filled Johan. As he watched the surgeon, he wondered if the man realized that the true Angel of Death had focused her beautiful eyes upon him, only to look away.

Mina sat in the uncomfortable pew, striving to pay attention to the Mass but could not keep her eyes from roaming. It was a smaller chapel than the one the Ma'am had attended in Charleston, but considerably nicer than any Mina had attended since. The choir was quite skilled and sounded wonderful; for a wonder, the voices of the congregation were perfectly in harmony, almost angelic. Emaline sat beside her, with eyes occasionally straying towards William. She was sweet on the boy...

No. Johan called him a man. Anyone who had seen the elephant was no longer a boy. She had to keep reminding herself of that.

Even among all the difficulties of war she felt so at home among Johan's mess. She had a tendency to think of them as her children, even though many were only a few years younger. They praised her cooking and appreciated her sewing; two of the boys had even offered to marry her when Johan died.

That idea made her smile. Johan was a good man who went out of his way to care for her. She felt a crooked grin cross her face...

No, no, those were not the kind of thoughts appropriate in a church!

Particularly not in front of the majority of the company. Even Major Wellman was here.

Why did Johan despise the surgeon so much? He was handsome and always courteous to her and the other laundresses. Always quick to pay his laundry bill and even consistently paid the girls a few pence extra. The major was in church every Sunday and he appeared to be a good, God-fearing man. Most importantly, he did not approve of slavery.

Or at least, he said he didn't. She knew he was no abolitionist. She had to agree with Johan that there was something about the man that she did not trust, she just could not pin down exactly what it was. For some reason she half suspected him of being a thief... and if he hadn't been an officer and a gentleman she would have been certain of it. Still, as thieves went, he seemed to be a decent sort. She had no doubt that Johan was a bit of a thief as well, but he was a thoroughly good man... so how was he any different than the Major?

Grinning, Emmanuel leaned forward and nudged Mina, pointing to the Captain. He was sleeping soundly, but with his head bowed low over his clasped hands it wasn't readily apparent. Trust a preacher to sleep through a sermon he himself probably had given a score of times on other occasions. Mina had to admit the man on the pulpit was a far from rousing speaker, even though his message was poignant and well thought out.

Johan puffed on his pipe and enjoyed the taste of fine tobacco as he listened to the singing coming from the chapel. It was pretty in its own way. They were making a joyful noise unto the Lord.

He had always enjoyed listening to the songs of a church. It was not the first time he had stood outside one looking in; he envied those within their faith. But he never felt welcome. It never felt quite right for him to step inside, as though there was something inherently wrong in his attendance. After all, he had killed, murdered even. He had stolen, been instrumental in adultery. That was three... there were no other commandments he could think of offhand. Just how many had he broken? Enough to make his soul permanently in danger, of that he was certain. Oh ,how he envied those with faith! They took comfort from their faith in difficult times. He lacked that.

Major Wellman was sitting with the rest of the officers. Seth and the rest of the mess were gathered close around Mina and the irritating red haired laundress. What was her name? Emaline, that was it. The young girl that had come looking for her brother, only to find his freshly dug grave. The Lakota had killed her family last fall and she had no one. So, naturally, Mina had adopted the child and brought her into her tent. Without Mina, the girl would probably be working in a house much like the one run by Kyrie by now.

Thinking of that tent... He needed to shorten the guide ropes. They stretched, and now seemed to be a bit too long.

As the chaplain began his sermon, Seth stood and walked out to join Johan. His face was twisted in anger, his fists clenched in barely contained rage. "I am so angry," the young man snarled. "I had to leave or I might accuse the surgeon of ungodly conduct. I know it is wrong to cast the first stone, I *know* it! But I'm so angry!"

Johan looked at Seth. "Even he needs God. He has a lot to be thankful for."

Seth snorted. "What does he have to be thankful for?"

"Kevin kept me from killing him."

Seth stared at him a long moment. "There is no God any longer. If there were, he would have struck that man down!"

Johan laughed. "You are a fool if you believe that. There is nothing wrong with religion. It gives hope to those who have none. Without faith in God, the helpless are denied even hope. Hope and prayer give a man a reason to keep going when all else is lost."

"Why do you never partake in services?" Seth asked innocently.

Johan grinned broadly. "I have no wish to tempt God should he change his mind and turn me into a pillar of fire. I am content to pray and listen from the safety of the door." Then he grabbed Seth by the collar and britches and pitched him into the chapel.

Seth stumbled over a chair and knocked over a flower arrangement. The chaplain looked up from his bible and changed the direction of his sermon. Seth apparently made an excellent example for the parable he was using.

Johan moved his queen, taking the rook and placing Seth into checkmate. It was a rudimentary chess board, the kind a bored soldier would make. The pawns were minie

152

balls, the rooks and knights were carved from a couple bits of hardtack. The bishops and queens were spent Burnside cartridges and the kings a pair of bad artillery fuses. It was a makeshift set of chess men but it did the job and was evidence of the creativity of bored soldiers. Seth had only recently learned the game, and he was an enthusiastic if unskilled player. Sebastian was more of a challenge and sat down on the cracker box across from Johan to try his hand at showing Johan how to lose. Johan smiled at the thought; the two best chess players in the company could barely read their names on a roster.

Seth had somehow begun a correspondence with one of the women of Kyrie's house. William had taken to memorizing the labels on cans and ammunition boxes as well as letters and poetry sent by the folks at home. Somewhere he had gotten the idea into his head to have a play for the whole regiment, and was getting men together to read from the English bard Shakespeare.

Johan looked down the trench line toward the sentries. August in Mississippi was unbearably hot, and the want of good water was beginning to tell on all of them. The shelter halves and rabbit holes burrowed into the hillside offered scant shade from the heat. Better than a third of the brigade was in hospital with dysentery or problems from too much heat. Unhealthy and boring, duty here was a challenge.

It was intriguing to man the defenses they had spent so long trying to take, but it was also sobering. The fortifications here had been as well built as any he had seen at Sevastopol and more ably defended. The attempts to take them by storm had been bloody affairs, and he still marveled that their losses had not been heavier.

Seth looked up from the letter he was composing. "Sergeant; what is a good French phrase to end a letter to a lady?"

"*Mai l'ombre de votre beauté n'accroissent jamais moins,*" Johan said without looking up from the game. Sebastian's move had been well made and he was going to lose a piece no matter how he countered it. The boy was learning.

"What does it mean?" Seth asked.

"Roughly it means 'may the shadow of your beauty never grow less.' That is the gist of it anyway."

Seth looked confused for a moment. "Sergeant, you want to spell that?"

Both Johan and Sebastian turned their heads to stare at him, unappreciative of the comment on their lack of literacy. Seth had failed to teach either man their letters, and he often reminded them that their inability hampered them.

"I didn't mean... I'm sorry, you two. I just don't know how to write it." And indeed, Seth looked apologetic. "Say, would you fellas prefer Much Ado About Nothing or Richard III? Will and I have been arguing about it for a week. We got seven guys to read whichever we choose."

Sebastian's look changed to one of confusion. "I never heard of either one."

Johan felt almost as foolish; his only knowledge of Shakespeare was Julius Caesar and the bit of Othello he had listened to in the barracks. "I know neither. Only a bit of Julius Caesar. Which will cheer us?"

Seth scratched his temple with the blunt end of his pencil. "Much Ado About Nothing is a comedy. But William has been quoting Richard III every chance he gets."

"I think we would prefer to smile than to hear tragedy," Johan said as he took a knight with his bishop.

Sebastian took the bishop with a flourish and then pushed a pawn to threaten his queen as Johan took the offending knight. "Sergeant, why did you join us?"

"It was the regiment being raised when I came to Fort Snelling." Johan said as he moved his queen to check Sebastian.

"No, no; I mean why did you join the Union?" Sebastian reached into his jacket to scratch at a grayback bite as he blocked the check.

Johan looked blankly at him for a moment. The boy was trying to distract him from the game. An interesting tactic. This boy was no fool. He was a cunning adversary. "There was a choice?" he asked, not needing an answer. "The Union fights to… how do I say? Maintain this country; the slavers fight to hold men in chains. I do not know how exactly this war came to be. But I think I understand why."

"Is it better than the old country?" Sebastian asked as Johan moved a bishop to defend his queen and Sebastian moved a rook to threaten his king.

Johan laughed as he moved his knight to checkmate the big man. "More than you can imagine. There is freedom here, to succeed or fail as you choose it. My only freedom in the old country was perhaps to make *Sergent Chef*. A man such as you or I might never be able to buy land to make ourselves any better than peasants." Johan chuckled at a thought. "This country is paying me for doing the only thing I have ever really been good at and the people back home are grateful for it."

Sebastian started to reset the board. "Do you think it any better in Minnesota than in the South?"

Johan did not hesitate. "Have you ever seen a slave auction?" he asked as he put the queen and bishops onto their proper spaces.

"No…" Sebastian seemed surprised by the question.

"That is the difference. And it is a poisonous one."

A long roll of drums brought Johan and the rest of the mess to their feet. They grabbed arms and accoutrements and rushed to their positions in the trenches. The drums meant the enemy was near; it meant battle.

The sun bore down on them, turning the earthworks into ovens. The heat was stifling and there was only the slightest breeze in the air. The men had fallen in with their gear, expecting an attack at any moment. No rations had been issued and water was getting low in canteens. Johan looked down the line and looked again under the head log out at the hills and trees in the distance. There was no enemy in sight; no sound of advancing columns of troops, and no sounds of guns being moved into position. Had some damnfool staff ass heard a rumor about enemy cavalry in the area and overreacted? If so, a long conversation with the idiot might be in order.

Johan stood and stretched, keeping his head below the level of the head log just in case he was wrong, and stopped abruptly. First Sergeant Tuttle from B Company was staggering along behind the line of entrenchments. The last he had seen the man he was in hospital with the dysentery, and he did not look that much better now. Tuttle almost literally fell in with his men and Johan could just hear his words.

"Heard you boys were going to have a scrap. If there's going to be a fight my place is here with you." He sounded weak but there was no doubt he was here for his men. Johan smiled slightly; up until now, he had never been all that impressed with the man.

"Johan. Where do you want this bread and soup?"

Johan turned to see Mina, Emaline and Sven standing there with a wheel cart holding a cauldron of soup, a score of loaves of fresh bread and a barrel of water. "Mina, you are an angel."

"I know," she said with a grin.

"Sergeant, just what are these civilians doing here?" the Captain demanded angrily as he came up the trench toward them.

"Feeding the masses, *mon capitaine*. How do you wish the food and water distributed, sir?" Johan asked with a grin.

Johan watched Mina give a ladle of soup a chunk of bread and a dipper of water to every man in the company. That woman was an angel. When they moved the wheel cart further along the works to B Company, Johan heard Tuttle wave off the food and water.

"Give it to the boys, they need it more than I do," he said. His voice was hollow and weak, and Tuttle himself was as pale as death. He was dying right there, and any who looked at him knew it. But had chosen his time and his place, and was here with his men. He was a good soldier, and Johan thought him a better man for spending his last hours with his men instead in of some hospital bed.

Two hours later Sergeant Tuttle was dead. Johan watched as six men from B Company and the Chaplain carried the limp body to a waiting ambulance.

It was almost dusk before the men were released from the line of battle and made their way back to camp. Many men made their way to the cemetery to pay their last respects to Sergeant Tuttle.

In the morning Sergeant Lane from B Company came into the camp at a run. "Steele, grab your mess and come running, you're needed at the hospital."

"Problem?" Johan asked.

"Trouble. We went to the hospital to get Tuttle's possessions and see that the package was sent home to his mother. The steward says there's nothing. We got paid only two weeks ago, right before he went to hospital. Then that Major threw me out saying I was trying to start trouble. Accused Wilks of trying to get…"

"I'll bring the whole company." Johan reached down and took hold of his accoutrements and hurriedly put them on.

"Good; I'm going to get the Colonel."

"He went down to Division Headquarters an hour ago with all the officers. Get the Sergeant Major instead." Johan tested the edge on his bayonet and sheathed it.

There were near to a hundred and fifty men from the regiment in front of the hospital when Major Wellman emerged from his quarters.

"Major, First Sergeant Tuttle had his belongings stolen." Sergeant Major Bianchi was a large man and he towered over the Major. He might well have been one of the oldest men in the regiment, a salt and pepper beard and mustache framed the face of a man who had spent his life working in the carpenter trade, enormous hands and a frame used to hard manual labor gave him an air of authority that was impossible to ignore. His voice was soft, but still carried an unspoken demand.

"What does this have to do with me, Sergeant Major?" He yawned as he spoke and looked at the men gathered behind the Sergeant Major. "Why are these men here?"

"To make certain his pay and belongings are sent home. Better than fifty dollars in gold coin and a fine gold watch are missing. The head steward said you had charge of the hospitals effects." The voice of the Sergeant Major carried clearly to all of the men and it was answered by a very hostile grumble.

Johan took his pipe out of his mouth and commented: "Sergeant Major; I have a rope." His voice carried and a score of men echoed his sentiments.

Major Wellman stepped forward. "Who said that? Sergeant Major, I demand that you disperse these men and bring that man up on charges." He was blustering, but could not hide the flash of fear behind his eyes

"Major, the effects will be produced or I will have these men search your quarters." The Sergeant Major stood his ground.

"Are you threatening me? I'm a Major!"

"No, sir. I'm not threatening you at all. The man with the rope is." His voice was steady and calm; he knew what he was about and was not intimidated by Wellman's rank. "Have you found an appropriate tree, Sergeant Steele?"

Johan smiled with relish. "Yes Sergeant Major, I have the perfect tree in mind. It is just tall enough."

"You cannot do this! I am an officer..."

"No, sir; you are a thief. You will produce the effects of First Sergeant Tuttle or I will leave you to the tender mercies of these men." The Sergeant Major was calm and in deadly earnest.

Major Wellman looked to the array of men in front of his quarters. It was hot, but the sweat beading on the man's brow was not caused by the heat. "I'll have the provost on you men for threatening a superior officer!"

Johan grinned broadly; and commented from the crowd. "I doubt it; you have to be able to talk to him to lodge a complaint." A slow rumble of murmurs came from the men assembled behind the Sergeant Major punctuated by several loud demands that they hang the man.

"Major Wellman, the Colonel is on his way here now. If I don't have First Sergeant Tuttle's effects by that time I shall be quite put out. I suspect the Colonel would order us to search your quarters anyway. I don't want to force him to give that order, because then it would look to the men like I didn't know my job and I don't like that idea. Now I know Sergeant Steele is an accomplished killer. I've watched him dispatch several men with his bayonet and he twice has been the hangman for the Provost Marshall. Do you want me to have Sergeant Steele pick a detail to apply some decoration to a tree?"

By the expression on his face, Major Wellman was boxed in and knew it. Johan smiled; these men were not armed past a few who carried bayonets, but they did not need arms to accomplish their task. If the Major resisted these men would tear his quarters apart and almost certainly him as well.

"I will get his box. I'm certain it was merely filed in the wrong slot."

"Major; I have checked the pay records; he had fifty dollars in gold coin on him when he came to hospital and a gold watch." The reminder was spoken in the same measured voice the Sergeant Major had used throughout.

Sergeant Lane chimed in. "Add ten dollars to that. Wilks paid off his chuck-a-luck debt."

The Major turned and went into his quarters emerging a few minutes later with a small wooden box and a ledger. "As I thought. It was filed in the wrong place."

"Of course it was. Now you will confess to the Colonel when he arrives…"

The Major was flushed and angry. "Damned if I will! I'm a Major in the…"

The Sergeant Major turned to Johan and interrupted the Major. "You have the rope ready Sergeant?"

"*Oui, Sergant Chef;* exactly short enough." Johan displayed the noose Kevin had just finished.

The Sergeant Major turned back to the Major who had gone completely ashen faced. "Now, Major. You will confess to the Colonel and resign your commission or Sergeant Steele and his merry band of cutthroats will see you swinging. Have I made myself clear?" And on the last sentence his voice rose to the volume of cannon shot.

"Yes." The Major almost whispered.

"Yes what?" The Sergeant Major demanded with a roar that carried across the town.

The Major jumped as though struck. "Yes, Sergeant Major."

The Sergeant Major looked at the Major with utter contempt in his eyes. "Good. Justice has been done." He turned to look at the men. " Sergeant Steele, put away that rope before the Colonel sees it and starts asking questions of the wrong man."

Mina stepped away from the fire; she was bone tired and more than ready for a good night of sleep. She was done for the day and could look forward to a profitable tomorrow. There were almost thirty dozen donuts in her bread truncheon, and a score of loaves of her sourdough bread that the men enjoyed so much. All told, she expected to earn better than fifteen dollars tomorrow from her baking. The men of the regiment would demolish the bread and donuts in minutes, and every officer in the regiment owed her at least two dollars for her laundry services. In fact, the Chaplain owed her near to ten. Yes, tomorrow would be a productive day.

She considered a moment. She had managed to hide away most of two hundred dollars. Johan knew she had her own money and he never asked about it. In fact, he had told her it was hers to spend as she saw fit. Yet she thought he had a good idea; the two of them would open a tavern and rooming house in Minnesota after the war. She would cook and clean and Johan would sell whiskey... though she suspected he would more likely drink a sizeable portion of it.

He had put away little of his own monies, spending most of it on liquor and tobacco. Money still meant little to the man, flowing readily through his fingers.

No, that wasn't really fair. In the years she had known him she couldn't think of a single occasion where she had seen him really fall down drunk, and she had seen him drink a lot of liquor. But his drinking was expensive and all that he had paid for his cognac added up to a hefty sum. So although he never drank himself silly or into a stupor, if he could bank that coin instead of drinking it away they would be better set than they were.

She had to admit that it irked her to be the only one putting away money. Johan didn't expect her monies to be his like most men would, and she liked that. He even insisted on calling it her money. If Mina chose to consider that money theirs instead of hers, then that was her choice.

She peered out of her tent at Johan sitting beside the fire. He had his customary bottle; she smiled sourly at that. He always managed to find a bottle of something somewhere. She wondered if he knew the significance of this town in her life? It was here they had boarded the northbound riverboat. She had left slavery here, never to suffer it again.

She had been afraid when Mr. Beasely had promised he would buy her. It might not have scared her quite so much if he had kept his hands to himself, but he hadn't. She had so desperately wanted to slap the man, but had dared not. The man had told her exactly what he was planning to do with her and the idea had revolted and frightened her.

The next morning Johan had handed over her papers and the papers of Mr. Beasely's two slaves Clara and Percy. She hadn't really understood how he gotten his hand on the documents… and she was certain she didn't really want to know. It had taken her only a few hours to create the letter that would help Percy and Clara to freedom. Johan had signed it and at St Louis she had watched the two head for Illinois.

She remembered asking what Mr. Beasely would say. The simple "Nothing," and the smile he gave her sent shivers down her spine whenever she thought of it.

She had never asked again. Mina didn't want to think of her Johan as a killer, but she knew in her heart of hearts that Mr. Beasely was dead by his hand. He must somehow have seen the man paw her. She tried never to think of such a thing, but still it haunted her conscience. She had once overheard Johan tell Seth that "No woman is worth dying for, killing for is another matter." Johan was willing to kill for her, to risk the law and his immortal soul. Knowing that gave her a higher opinion of herself; she was worth at least the life of a rich Alabama businessman. At the same time, it was a sobering responsibility, as though the blood were partly on her hands as well.

She knew Johan had set three people, including her, onto the road of freedom. He lacked the prejudice so prevalent that it wasn't even admitted as wrong. Johan judged people as individuals by their merits and failings instead of by the color of their skin. He didn't try to impress people. She didn't think he really cared what people thought of him, and wasn't sure he even liked people in the first place. What she did know was that she had come to love him, and that the war had not diminished that love. If anything she loved him more intensely. It wasn't the kind of love from a storybook, but a simple and practical love. *Real* love.

Johan looked at the note that Sven handed him and put down his bottle of whiskey. "What is this?" Sven knew he couldn't read.

"The lady Kyrie handed it to me and said to put it in your hands, and to let nobody else to see it."

"What were you doing at her house?" Johan asked as he turned the note over in his hand; it was heavy.

"Delivering a note to the woman Seth been gossiping with." The boy sounded so proud.

"I think Mina told you to stay away from that place," he said with a quirk of his mouth.

"She not know. Besides, how else Seth gonna get his letters from the pretty lady?"

Johan laughed. "Mina will tan your hide if she finds out."

"She don't know everything," Sven said with a smile. Then he saw the look on Johan's face and stopped. "Leastways I don't think she knows everything."

Johan tore open the envelope and saw Sven's eyes widen in surprise as the two twenty dollar gold eagles fell from it. Two sets of eyes stared at the gold coins for a moment.

"Them what I think they is, Massa Steele?" Sven asked ,wide-eyed.

Johan cuffed him lightly on the head. "Do not call me 'Massa,' and yes, they are. Come along." He stood up from the fire, examining the coins as he did so. The boy knew all the ways around the pickets; he would lead Johan to the House of Kyrie without the necessity of a pass.

Johan reflected later he was going to have to remember the route Sven took. Easy enough to follow even with only a sliver of the moon to light their way, and it took them less than half an hour to reach the house. Sven led Johan to a back door that led into the kitchen. The boy knocked twice, and then three more times in quick succession.

An enormous black man answered the door, and when he spoke it was the sound of gravel grating. "You brought him. Good. The missus will see him now."

The man was only a few inches taller but easily forty pounds heavier than Johan though there little if any fat on him. A large cudgel leaned, easy to hand, next to the door. Though Johan doubted the man would need such a thing. With his size, massive build and the dark look on his face only a fool would fight the man.

The big man showed Johan and Sven through the kitchen and up a narrow flight of stairs. The house was well built and the rooms were spacious; the construction was such that Johan could not hear the noises he expected to hear in such a place.

The massive black man stopped at an equally-massive iron bound oak door, knocked lightly, then entered. The room was lit only by a pair of lamps and it was dim.

The room recalled his youth in the Amsterdam brothel. It was as he remembered Madam Melinda's personal bedroom to be; opulent, with red fabric everywhere. He had been in that room only twice. In both cases it had been to remove and dispose of a body. None of the girls had been permitted in there; it had been the madam's private room, her escape from the rest of the world, and she had spared no expense in furnishing it. Kyrie had done the same to this room, and the similarities were disturbing.

A small woman lay in the enormous four poster bed, bandages concealing grievous injuries. One emerald green eye was completely swollen shut, and the other stared hatefully out at him from beneath a bloody bandage. She might have been pretty before the beating; now she was one continuous bruise. Kyrie sat in an exquisitely carved rocking chair beside the bed.

"Johan. Good, the boy found you." Kyrie spoke in Dutch with a voice full of pent up anger.

"What do you want me to do, Kyrie?" Johan asked as he looked back to see the big black man leave the room.

Kyrie reached out and clasped the bandaged woman's hand. "Do you not see her? Her name is Maxine, and her husband almost killed her last night. She has three broken ribs and a broken arm. The doctor thinks she will never hear from her right ear again, and she may be blind in her right eye as well. He beat her almost to death and when Erik tried to stop it the bastard pulled a pistol and threatened to shoot him. He only left when he thought he had killed her." Kyrie was calm as death, the Angel of Death incarnate, but barely contained rage simmered just beneath her words.

"She is one of yours?" Johan asked.

"Does it matter?" Her eyes were the color of ice.

Johan recoiled unconsciously from the look she gave him. "No, no. Who is he?"

"A quartermaster named Martin. Kill him, but make him pay first. Do you understand?" Kyrie spoke carefully, leaving no room for misunderstanding.

"Then we will be even?" Johan asked quietly.

She stood up and slapped him hard. "You son of a bitch. We shall never be even. But this will make things right between us. The forty dollars is to hire help if you need it. He is a big man, so you might. Now get the hell out of my house."

Johan rubbed his cheek and bowed slightly to her. "You will hear of it." He took Sven by the shoulder and left.

When they stepped into the night Sven stopped Johan. "Why did she slap you?"

Johan sighed and knelt before the boy. How to tell him that he would gladly kill for that woman? "We were friends once. I hurt her very badly. I did not mean to, but intentions many times count for nothing. I owe her for that hurt. The woman in the bed was hurt very badly, and she wants me to bring justice to the man that caused it."

"You gonna kill him?" the boy asked seriously.

"Yes." Johan's answer was quick and cold.

"I'm glad. He shouldn't have hurt Ms. Maxie that way." There was a vehemence there that surprised him.

Johan looked into the dark eyes of the boy and wondered just what he had seen in his short life. Perhaps it would be better if he did not know. "Sven, promise me that you will say nothing of this to Mina or to anyone."

"Only if I can help; I like Ms. Maxie. She's my friend." Sven looked into Johan's eyes as he spoke. There was a coldness there that did not belong behind the eyes of a child; this was a man in a child's body.

Johan considered a moment. "Go get me William and Kevin, tell them to come with full kit and have one of them bring my gear. Do you know that rebel cap and jacket we gave you? Bring them as well. We have dark work to do tonight."

Johan looked at the two men Sven had brought to him as he put on his gear and checked his rifle. Kevin and William were good men to have with you in a fight, and had proven so on the field of battle. But they were also honest men with real morals and a deep seated sense of justice. The war had hardened the hearts of both men, but it had not darkened them. Kevin had shown that he was willing to skirt the law if occasion required it, and neither had any patience for those that might hurt a woman.

They had been the only two of his mess he would consider for work such as this. While Bryce and Sebastian both would have willingly accompanied him on this task ,he did not trust Sebastian to keep his mouth shut. Bryce would not easily hide things from his *copain* either, so word would get out. Emmanuel would also have willingly joined his little detail but he was a touch too naïve and would have required too much convincing. Nate and Seth were not options at all, as both were far too innocent and Seth probably would have attempted to reform the man they were going to hang.

No, William and Kevin would do nicely. Kevin would be eager and William would keep his mouth shut. But most importantly neither would have qualms about what they were about to do.

The two men simply looked to him, awaiting their orders. "We are about to do mischief tonight. If you do not feel right about it or do not trust me, now is the time to speak of it. I will think no less of you." Johan spoke very carefully so there would be no doubt of his words.

Their answer was simple silence while they waited his command. Sven smiled at him with a grin of pure malice; the grin was not directed at him but at the man who was to die tonight.

"I will do what is required this eve. If you are pressed, tell them I was in command and you were following my orders."

All three men nodded their agreement. Without another word Johan led his detail into the darkness with Sven guiding them toward the quarters of the condemned man. They were going to arrange the judgment of a man by God. He suspected this quartermaster named Martin who beat women would find Johan's judgment rather harsh, and if he were to learn a lesson on the way, all the better.

Though he would not profit from the lesson for very long.

Outpost Duty

Outpost and picket duty was a fact of life for the Civil War soldier. Fords, bridges and important locations had to be garrisoned to protect them from raiders. It was a duty that was often looked forward to, as it took the men away from the main army and into the relative peace of the country-side. Although that peace was often shattered without notice by a raid by the enemy.

ohan leaned back against the tree. He looked out across the river and enjoyed what he saw: beautiful land with ample timber bordering both banks of the river. Oddly, the roads running on both sides highlighted the scenery. This river crossing was well defended by the little outpost. The ruined mill still had all four stone walls and even part of the roof. The Cooperage stood duty as a small hospital, and the inn as a home for the civilian family operating the ferry.

The family that ran the ferry was staunch Unionist - so long as the garrison were US soldiers. He rather suspected their loyalties would lie with whatever flag was flown. That aside, Johan thought they were decent enough people, if a touch strange.

Seven children and three adults made a full house no matter the size. The children stayed away from the soldiers, unless one wandered too close to the inn. Then they wanted to see the man's rifle, look into his haversack, and know everything there was to know about the soldier. If the soldier was a good storyteller, they would pester him at the picket post next to the road. The wife and two eldest daughters were competent cooks and were more than willing to bake bread in trade. A couple of rations of salt pork guaranteed a man several loaves of excellent if grainy bread. It was a far cry from Mina's, but it was a preferable alternative to hardtack.

The wife was a harsh looking woman who looked to be in her forties, but Johan suspected the children may well have aged her. She had a pleasant voice and a polite manner, always very careful not to offend. Her husband was an irascible and argumentative sort; how no one had taken enough offense to kill him amazed Johan. Yet he was a hard worker with a wife and children he did a splendid job of caring for and supporting. The oldest girl was perhaps a pretty thirteen, with three younger sisters ranging down to five or six. The three boys... he figured the oldest at a young fifteen, and the other two around eight or nine. The oldest wanted to be a soldier. He was certainly strong and mature enough that the Rebels would gladly take a boy like him faster than he could volunteer. But he stayed with his family because he knew they needed him.

What were their names? Johan had to stop and think for a few minutes. Names meant little to him. He rarely remembered them unless his mind told him they were important to him. And even then he would forget them given half a chance. Edward... Edward Meyer, was the father. The wife was... was... come to think of it, had he ever heard the woman's name? Katie, Kathleen perhaps? The girls were Leslie, Megan, Candice and Anna, though he wasn't certain which was which. He suspected Leslie to be the eldest one. The boys were Daniel, Morgan and Carson. Still, though he could not name them, Johan had to admit he liked them all.

The company lived in a smattering of dog tents, a couple wedges and even a Sibley tent that Johan had stolen from the back of a baggage wagon in the train of one of the new batteries. If that Sibley managed to stay lost long enough for that battery to be reassigned - or better yet to be sent home on furlough - he might just see that Sibley in the hands of the ladies. It was roomier than his old tent and frankly easier to set.

Their camp was arrayed a hundred or so yards above the river. There were no real earthworks here, though a levy to the north of the mill might be called that by anyone attacking from the river. This little valley was beautiful, with fresh flowers blooming and the trees full. It was a fresh and welcome change from the stale air of the city and entrenchments around it. He lit his pipe and let the place talk to him. There was just enough a breeze to cool the area and move the trees. He had always liked the sound of the wind, and it didn't matter if it was in the desert or through the trees. He remembered a fellow Legionnaire calling the wind the breath of life. There was wisdom in such words.

Johan had to try very hard to remember his parents. A father who always worried about money, and his mother… the only memory he had of her was of soft arms. He remembered the work house and the other children, some weak and hopeless, others who were bullies. He hadn't been one of the bullies, not really. Instead he had hurt the bullies. They were cowards and so easy to frighten. And once frightened, they were no longer bullies and easily controlled. It may have been his actions towards the bullies that attracted Madame Melinda.

In his early days in the Legion he discovered he could actually do something very well. He had always liked his knife but the Legion introduced him to the bayonet. They trained him to use it, to kill a man face to face while looking into his eyes. Looking into the eyes of the man you were killing *meant* something. The Legion had also taught him to use the musket, and later the rifle to kill at range, and he was good at those as well. Everything the Legion had taught him to do, he did well. He was good at hurting people, he always had been. In the Legion he had acquired a fascination with death; it was so easy to end a man's life. Yet at the same time man was inherently tough, and given a chance a body would fight tooth and nail for life.

There had been other men like him in the Legion, men he understood and who understood him. Men like Remi, Sarro, Maurice, Thomas and Enrique. Of them all only Remi still lived and even Remi might have fallen by now.

The Legion had been the only place he had ever really felt comfortable, surrounded by men just like him. He learned everything he could from those around him, and he applied it with real skill.

Perhaps it was the power of life and death that was so intoxicating. Perhaps that was why he chose to kill. It was so easy, easier than being around them. He often felt frustrated and angry for no particular reason, like there was something he was missing and he couldn't find it. He had tried sex and religion; neither filled the emptiness. This brought him closer to the Angel of Death, made him like her in an odd sort of way. It was one of the few things that actually frightened him. He wasn't afraid of death - he almost relished the moment when the Angel would come for him, when he might meet her. But he feared what would come after.

Johan took a long look at his pipe and listened to the wind and the sound of the river below him. Outpost duty was the kind of duty he preferred. No polish or inspections, just real soldiering; that, along with the beauty of the place, was what he liked. It was also a bit of a relief to be away from the city and any questions that might be asked about his actions on that dark night a week ago.

It was a real pity what had happened to that officer; men should not have to die that way. To be caught by Rebel guerillas and strung up, though not before they had broken almost every bone in the man's body, that was no way for a man to die. It had been a real tragedy. Truly tragic... really.

Johan felt himself grin evilly. Justice had been done.

Seth and Joshua were at the post closest to him overlooking the road. They were a good hundred feet above that road. It was always considerably cooler in the camp, outright cold sometimes in the morning, and so Johan preferred to sleep at this post. The Captain had given him command of this chain of posts and whoever had initially decided to use this place had an eye for good solid defensive terrain. A company could hold this place against a regiment, and a regiment…well, a regiment could hold the whole damned Rebel army.

Johan looked down at the white canvas that identified the camp and studied the place. The mill was built in such a way that it was all but impenetrable to attack. Backed up against the giant rock that was the bluff and at the apex of a curve, it was most of four stories tall and commanded the crossing like a castle out of old times. It was situated in such a way that at most one gun could be wheeled into action against it, and only then if the enemy manhandled it into place on the shelf overlooking the river a couple hundred yards to the north. Those gunners would be easy pickings for any man who knew how to shoot, though, and there was no doubt that the men of this company knew how to shoot. To the south the road was lower and easily commanded from the upper stories of the mill. The stout stone walls would be proof against any rifle fire. It was truly a good place to defend.

There was another post with William and Kevin a few hundred paces further along the bluff, positioned so as to see anyone trying to sneak around the mill's crossing point. Emmanuel and Nate were another hundred paces past that, watching a foot path that led down to the crossing. There were perhaps twenty pickets on his side of the line; no Rebel guerrillas were likely to surprise the company.

He wished Mina and Sven were here. But there was no need to bring along the camp followers for a week of outpost duty. He missed her cooking, her presence, and above all he missed her spirit and that ever-present smile that he had come to love so much. There had been camp followers in the Legion, laundresses and whores but they were not these women. There was Marie, the drummer Blair's mother, a fetching farm wife of perhaps forty. Some might say she was too old to follow the army... but they would not say so after watching her move about the regiment. Her love of her son was an intriguing thing to watch. It made him wish he had known his own mother. Yet she did not know Blair had dropped his drum and taken up a rifle at both Iuka and the assault on Vicksburg. Blair was a good man from good stock, and even his mother should no longer see him as a boy.

There was Deelia, who had joined the regiment as a laundress but who spent all of her time in the hospital doing the work of an angel in that horrid place. The two young ones, Emaline and Elissa, were both too pretty and far too naïve to be among so many men. He liked to look at them though. They were no Mina, but they were pleasing enough to the eye.

He shook his head and tried to get the faces of women from his mind. He had to pay attention to his surroundings. It was easy to become distracted in this peaceful spot and forget that there was an enemy out here who would kill you as soon as look at you.

Joshua stumbling out of the trees at near to a dead run brought Johan out of his thoughts in an instant. "Sergeant, a wagon's coming down the road with a pair of horseman on the flanks!" His whisper was frantic and filled with the excitement that comes from being in enemy territory.

Johan got to his feet and slung his rifle. "Let us see."

He jogged up the hill to the giant rock Joshua and Seth held down. It really was an awesome rock; easily three times the size of the ship that had carried him across the Atlantic. The view from it was truly spectacular.

Seth knelt behind a tree, using a low branch to steady his rifle; he was taking careful aim on the driver of the wagon. Johan put his hand on Seth's shoulder. "Hold, that is a woman. See her dress? And those are boys on mules, so are not Rebel cavalry. Refugees, I think. They have to stop at the post on the road. You two watch the road in case they are a distraction."

Johan moved to the edge of the enormous rock and looked down at the wagon and escort below him. He had been right; the woman looked to be the mother of the two boys sitting on the mules. They were just trying to get across the river.

Johan waved the to Joshua and Seth and went back to his tree and the spectacular view it held. There was no need to call out the reserve for a refugee family.

Johan mused at the life of a soldier at war. There were really four types of soldier in any army and this one was no exception. Most were men who just wanted to survive and did their level best to do so. Most of the men in the company were of that class. Then there were those like Seth, who believed all of the patriotic nonsense that had started the war off in the first place and honestly felt they were doing right. Of course there were the shirkers and cowards who were always absent as soon as they were needed.

The smallest number were the stone cold killers; the men with cold eyes who seem to enjoy the killing and revel in the death around them. Johan had watched a couple of men file notches in the stocks of their rifles after Iuka, and the Dakota boy, Little Foot, took scalps at every opportunity. Johan thought them a class of man a little mad; but who was he to judge?

He remembered something Remi had said; the quickest way to ruin a soldier was for him to fall in love. Whether a whore, the wife of an officer or the beautiful daughter of a rich man. Johan smiled at the thought. He was happy to have found a good woman and to let her love him.

Johan felt the pressure in his kidneys that told him it was time to empty them. There was a tree he could use a few yards up the slope. As he buttoned up his trousers he saw Seth running full tilt down the slope towards him. "Trouble, Sergeant, no refugees this time. At least fifty men, infantry I think." Seth was excited but not noticeably scared.

Johan slung his rifle again and started up the hill behind Seth. As soon as they reached Joshua the enemy was visible through the trees. They were drawn up watching the road and waiting for some sort of signal. Johan looked hard. He thought Seth was right; about fifty men, no more.

"Seth, hightail it to the Captain. Tell him what you saw. I would say they are about six hundred yards out. Go, at the double quick." Johan did some quick math in his head. "They have no chance of pushing us off this rock. Not enough men."

Seth took off at a good run, quickly weaving his way through the trees. He was a good runner and used to maneuvering through the hills and woods around his house.

Johan pushed Joshua to an outcropping of rock. "Fire only when I tell you."

Joshua nodded that he understood. He settled behind the rock resting his rifle in a notch in the rock as he did so. Johan moved a few paces closer to the edge of the wood and studied the men he saw waiting there. They were certainly Rebels and from the way they stood and waited

179

they were not concerned. Yet they had to know that they had been seen and that the reserve was likely moving to reinforce the pickets.

The distinctive sound of the recall being sounded brought his head around. Seth had gotten there quicker than he had expected. But why had the Captain sounded the recall? Johan moved the seventy or so paces to where he could see the camp.

"Here come Kevin and Will!" Joshua yelled to let Johan know. "Oh damn, here comes Johnny!"

William and Kevin had heard the recall; but so had the Rebels. That meant they had been waiting for something. The recall meant no one was advancing to deal with them, so they had to know fifty men were not enough... unless there was a second force on the other side of the picket line.

Johan put his hand out to stop them. "Boys, stop. We are staying on this hill. Emmanuel and Nate should be only..."

As if on cue they came jogging through the woods. "Hey, Sergeant, ugly is a coming and he brought lots of friends!" Nate said with a worried look.

"What?" Johan asked not understanding what he meant. Nate stopped and took a breath. "About a company of Secesch, fifty, maybe seventy five men, come up from the south to try and grab the company. The rest of the pickets hauled down the path to the mill. It was closer for us to come this way."

Johan cursed quietly. This was why he was only a Sergeant and the Captain was a Captain. "We stay on the hill, it is quite a climb to get up here and if we are shooting they might think twice. Joshua, where are they?"

"Coming down the road, as easy as you please." Joshua was taking careful aim as he spoke.

"Are they sending any skirmishers this way?" Johan asked.

"Not a one. They're almost to the inn. Can I let one of 'em have it?"

"No, we wait. They heard the recall and think we all are down in the mill by now. No need to let them think different." Johan scratched his chin then absently rubbed the scar on his throat.

Nate looked at him. "Sergeant, I really don't like the idea of a prison camp."

"I like the idea of dying less." William said with a grimace.

"One group is below us by the inn, the other must be by the camp," Johan said past a scowl. "I hope none of you left anything you want to see again. Nate, you and Emmanuel could see our camp from your post, yes?"

"Yea, but not the mill," Emmanuel said with a confused look. "We gonna take on a company by our lonesome?"

"No, we are going to kill a few of them and then come back to this rock. If they want us, they will have to work at it. This is a good spot; hard to get at from below if someone is shooting. We sell ourselves as soldiers; hard. The Captain will appreciate it, as will the rest of the company." Johan looked at them all carefully. Would they fight? Yes.

Joshua stood up. "I want to…"

Johan interrupted him. "No, I want Nate and Emmanuel here with you. I do not want to come back here to find a Rebel waiting for me. Hold this place and wait for us. You will hear us volley and then we may come running. So look before you shoot. I do not want to be penned up here if we can still move. If they do not know where we are they

181

will not easily take us." He looked to his men. "Do you all understand?"

All nodded. It was going to be a long day. Johan checked his rifle, took a quick look at his bayonet. "We go."

William and Kevin followed him along the ridge. The thick strip of timber that was the edge of the outpost was a gift from God. It was impossible to see them from below and it was steep enough that climbing up to it under fire would be quite unhealthy. As they came to Nate and Emmanuel's post the small valley spread out below them.

There were easily a hundred men down there at the edge of the camp. They were most of four hundred yards distant, but in plain sight from their position. Rebel soldiers were busily rooting through the tents. An officer and an enormous sergeant were approaching the mill under a flag of truce. They would demand the Captain surrender his command; Johan was not worried. The Captain was in a strong position and he could make them pay dearly to get into the mill.

The Rebel officer and his giant of a sergeant returned to the camp. Johan could almost hear the command to form up; they were preparing to attack. Damn fools.

"Aim at the officers and sergeants," Johan said with an evil grin. "Wait till they start forward, then shoot."

The enemy moved forward and the tiny group volleyed as one man. Johan felt the recoil as his round went downrange. The officer fell, as did the enormous sergeant. The three of them reloaded as rapidly as they could and watched the fight unfold before them. Puffs of white smoke showed that the men were firing from the mill. The Rebels were likely attacking from the other side of the mill as well.

Johan spotted a group of Rebels turn and face them.

182

"Here comes a volley!" William shouted as he squeezed behind a tree and Kevin made himself a close personal friend of the earth. Johan slid behind a tumbled down tree and knelt as he finished reloading.

A bit of bark spit into his face as a bullet dislodged it. "You two alright?" Johan barked.

"Those bastards can shoot!" Kevin replied.

"So can we!" William replied.

"One more volley then we move back to the rock in skirmish order," Johan ordered.

Johan looked from the bullet pocked walls of the mill to the wrecked camp. Most anything of value was gone. Seth complained about the loss of his book and his writing kit, William was whining about the loss of his Shakespeare, and Kevin was powerful upset about a broken bottle of bourbon. Admittedly, that last had been a crime. Almost every man of the company had lost something from the hastily looted camp, and there was not a stitch of canvas in sight. That left just two tents in the company, his own *tent d'abri* and a tent fly the men had used to cover the rations inside the mill.

The important thing was that no one had been hurt, the only casualty Bryce's hat, which had lost its brim to a bullet. The banner that Bryce and Sebastian had hung from the upper story amused Johan to all ends. Nate read it to him. "Caskets two dollars. Prayers free."

Johan laughed. "Seth, tell me again what the Captain said when they demanded we surrender."

Seth looked very serious and then in his best approximation of the Captain's voice said, "'Sir, may I have the honor of your name?'" It was a good approximation.

"And the Reb Major said, 'Why should I give you my name?' and you know what the Captain said?" Seth paused for dramatic effect and in a very serious voice. "'So that my men might properly mark your grave; you have my answer, sir.' You should have seen the look on that man's face! Then Bryce shouted down from the window, 'Caskets, two dollars.' Oh, it was perfect! You never seen such a thing."

They all grinned; the Captain went up another notch in all of their eyes.

"Is the Meyer family alright?" Emmanuel asked.

"They're fine, spent the fight in the back half of the inn; never saw them until after the Rebs hightailed it." Seth grinned somewhat sheepishly. "You should have heard Mr. Meyer cursing; the Rebs stole both his mules and knocked holes in his barn for firing ports. The man was fit to be tied. He's already asking the Captain if he can get compensation for his mules."

Kevin laughed. "All that matters is they're all fine." Johan nodded in agreement, as did every man in the mess.

"Which of you shot that Major? That took the fight right out of them." Seth asked.

"Kevin; I missed." Johan said quietly looking at the two of them as he spoke.

"The Captain wants them mentioned in dispatches!" Seth grinned broadly.

North Georgia, 1864

Cavalry raids against lines of communication and supply depots were an effective way for the Confederacy to strike at the US military. Strong garrisons and active patrols were a necessity to fight such. However, unlike Confederate Cavalry, irregular partisans and guerrillas left their own mark upon the area. The soldiers of both armies generally despised the men who participated in such fighting, because their victims were all too often the innocent.

Seth looked ahead at the long column of men and guns winding along the narrow track. The day was chill and held the promise of rain in the air. The regiment was moving quickly, though at nowhere near the pace they had set on the way to Vicksburg. They'd been marching since an hour or so after dawn, but the march was almost leisurely after their veteran furlough. Only the professional complainers were making a fuss about it.

God, but it had been good to see the family again, and the chance to get some of the people they had collected out of harm's way had been priceless. Though he knew some were already missing Emaline. They had tried their best to leave Sven in Minnesota, only to find the boy on the boat with them on the way back to the war. There had to be a story there worth something. The boy was bold, brave enough for any in the regiment. The company, to a man, were his friends and he refused to let his friends go back to war without him. He was one of them, whether they liked it or not. Some of the boys laughed at him because he was black and not well educated... it was foolish. Sergeant Steele had called such attitudes asinine, and he was right. He and Mrs. Mina, to name just two, were spending great effort educating him.

It had taken only minutes to break camp this morning. "Tent d'Abri" as Sergeant Steele called them, came down and were rolled into blanket rolls or folded into knapsacks. Two years ago they never could have gotten the regiment onto the road in twenty minutes, but now the men were hardened campaigners used to the rigors of military life. There was no baggage but what was carried on the backs of soldiers, and the only vehicles a single commissary wagon, and ambulance, and Mrs. Mina's cart which was chock full of ammunition.

Seventy-odd pounds spread among blankets, rations and weapons. It really was amazing what a man pared down to when he knew there was marching ahead of him. About a third of the men still had their knapsacks. The rest had chosen the simple blanket roll. A few men carried two blanket rolls, or their knapsack and a blanket roll, but the majority wore that simple blanket roll that looked like a mule collar. What a picture they must have made, uniform only in their greatcoats and filthy appearance.

None but three men in the ranks of the company had the fancy cap of the eastern armies. Slouch hat or abused Hardee hats shielded ears and neck far better than the flimsy visor on a forage cap. Seth couldn't recall ever having been issued one of the ridiculous looking things. Just those dress hats back at Fort Snelling, and most of those were no longer even vaguely fancy.

Even at the route step the men found themselves in unison; a rhythmic beat as several hundred left feet came down at once. It was easier that way. No one stepped on the heels of the man in front of him. And the sound of so many marching feet was oddly comforting, with the occasional added sound of the battery wheels creaking just ahead of them. The men were no longer singing or even really carrying on conversations. Instead, there was the occasional muted voice or conversation.

Bryce and Sebastian both snored as they slept ahead of him; Seth marveled that men could sleep while they marched. Quite a few had become quite adept at it. Seth had never tried it. Some said those who "sleep marched" weren't actually sleeping at all, but Seth knew different; he'd seen Bryce, Sebastian, Sergeant Steele and others close their eyes and catch some sleep as they marched.

How they never stumbled or fell over was a mystery to him, and how they received any rest from such a practice Seth had no idea.

The scent of Sergeant Steele's tobacco occasionally wafted back to him as the man absently puffed on his pipe. Others read their testaments or letters from home and he even knew of a couple who could write a letter on the march. The how of it confounded him though.

Nate and Emmanuel carried on a whispered conversation about how to spend their pay after the war. They seemed to think that if they pooled their monies they would have enough to buy better than one hundred acres. Emmanuel planned to make banjos and fiddles to supplement their income and Nate wished to raise goats. Seth debated injecting the idea that cattle were a better breed of livestock, but suspected the two wouldn't appreciate his eavesdropping on their conversation.

Instead he pulled his testament from the folds of his blanket roll and fished out the last letter he had received from Carlie and looked at the passage underneath the letter: *"He is dressed in a robe dipped in blood and his name is the word of God. The armies of heaven are following him."*

Perhaps it meant something that he had folded it into Revelation. Were these the end times? There were certainly enough signs that might point to such being the case. Seth unfolded the letter and began to read it again. Carlie's words were so precious to him; a taste of home and of civility. Men were not trying earnestly to kill one another in her letters. Instead, news of a new mare or one of mother's pies winning a prize emerged from the paper. They were a touch of life away from the war, a reminder of what he was fighting for. When she spoke of the bad things that happened around home she was careful to voice them in such a way as not to worry him. When he read those letters he imagined her voice reading to him.

It was a bit of peace.

Joshua elbowed him. "Seth, you think we'll have a fight when we get there?"

Seth grimaced, lowering the letter. "The Captain says we have easy garrison work ahead of us with detachments guarding trains and bridges. When Sherman makes the big grab of prisoners, we'll likely guard some of them on their way to Rock Island or Camp Chase. Sergeant Steele says we'll probably have a sharp scrap or two with raiders and guerrillas."

"You ever heard of Allatoona?" Joshua asked.

Seth snorted, "I barely even heard of Vicksburg before we went there!"

Seth concentrated on the doll he was whittling and tried to keep the fear out of his throat. Sergeant Steele knew what he was about. He shouldn't worry. He felt himself look around at the forest clearing.

The space was not more than seventy paces wide. A narrow but fast flowing stream flowed along one side, and a deeply rutted road passed through the center. The wedge tent the Sergeant had "found," plus three dog tents stood in a neat row fifteen or so paces from the edge of the road opposite the stream. Mrs. Mina's small two-wheeled Mormon cart sat a few paces from the wedge tent with a fifth shelter half hung off the back end. A mule busily munched grass a few yards from the cart, and two campfires illuminated the clearing in the dusk.

Sergeant Steele, wearing a worn sack coat and weather beaten Hardee hat sat on an empty cracker box smoking his pipe. His rifle stood close to hand with a fixed bayonet. Most of the regiment had the new M1861 Springfield, but the Sergeant had managed to keep hold of his M1841 with its vicious-looking sword bayonet. Somehow it fit the man.

Occasionally the Sergeant stirred the fire, checking some sweet potatoes and husks of corn in the ashes as he did so. A battered coffeepot sat in the midst of the coals. The scents coming from the fire were oddly comforting, coffee with a hint of cedar.

A group of a dozen Rebel cavalrymen who had been forced to politely surrender their arms and their mounts lounged around another fire twenty feet from Sergeant Steele. Occasionally some of the prisoners looked sullenly at the Sergeant and the men lounging about the camp. Joshua had a ragged copy of Harpers Ferry from March of '62.

While Seth absently whittled that stick, he whistled quietly. Their rifles were also close to hand, although unlike the Sergeant their bayonets were absent. Seth felt that the whistling relaxed and calmed him; Amazing Grace was one of his favorite hymns, and it sounded as beautiful whistled as sung.

"Halloo the fire!" A voice announced from the woods. No one was surprised.

The Sergeant didn't look up from what he was doing. "Come in if you like, swinging if you have a mind to. Coffee is on." He didn't yell - didn't even seem to raise his voice - but his words carried easily across the clearing.

A detail of infantry led by a corporal, carrying supplies and leading a mule, walked into the clearing. They were clearly bound for a unit closer to the Rebel lines. All except the Corporal had their rifles slung over their shoulders; each man carried a full burlap bag and led a heavily laden mule. They looked tired and worn, evidence of a long march.

"Steele, why are you cooking? Your wife quit you?" The Corporal asked with a lopsided grin.

Sergeant Steele was still lithe and spare of build with a heavy beard concealing his features. He hadn't changed much in the years since he had wintered at the farm with Seth's family. Seth could see those intense gray eyes looking back at the Corporal from under the brim of his hat. Most of the men called him Steele or Johan now, but not Seth, he just couldn't bring himself to that level of familiarity very often.

Sergeant Steele smiled as he took the pipe from his mouth and emptied the spent tobacco onto the ground. "Nay, Corporal, the wife is getting a well deserved sleep." His voice was smooth with more of a hint of an accent than usual. Seth wondered if he had snuck a few more sips than he should have from that bottle of Scotch he had acquired from that Reb cavalry Captain. "Any more of you Iowa boys coming up the road?"

"No, we're it. We're bringing up some grub. It's mostly onions and desiccated vegetables - or desecrated, depending on who you ask. There's some turnips thrown in for variety. Your woman learn you to read yet?" Corporal Russel tossed his knapsack to the ground and settled beside it as he spoke. He let out an audible sigh of relief as he dropped his burden. Obviously footsore and tired, he pulled off his brogans and looked forlornly at Seth through a hole in the sole. The other men of his detail settled around the fire as the Corporal poked a finger through the hole in the bottom of his brogan and wiggled it.

The Sergeant fished a tin of tobacco out of his bedroll. "She tries, still mostly just chicken scratches to me. She did well enough cleaning up my English."

He paused long enough to look at Seth who was still absently whistling as he whittled. "Call them in, Seth."

Seth whistled shrilly, then went back to his whittling. A moment or two later a pair of soldiers entered the clearing from the other side of the stream, hopping across it. They carried their rifles casually in their arms and waved cheerfully at the Rebel prisoners.

The Corporal chuckled. "Not a trusting sort, are you, Steele? So why are those Rebs giving you such nasty looks?"

Sergeant Steele smiled as he stirred the coals with a stick again. "I told them if you were friends of theirs that William would take one of them with the first volley and I would bayonet the first one I reached. That calmed them some. I figured Kevin would nail the first Reb he out of the trees. Kevin is a rare fine shot."

The Corporal reached for the coffee pot and poured a cup for each man in his detail.

"Another three, four miles isn't it?' Sergeant Steele asked.

"I figure closer to five, to our company. We can make it by midnight or so. The moon will make the trip a bit easier." The Corporal said as he blew on his coffee to cool it.

"I'll take Kevin and Seth and have these Secesh horse thieves carry those bags for you. That way you and your boys can relax a bit on the way back to your Company. These Secesh won't mind a bit of a detour on their way to Rock Island. They can use a walk, they've been riding too long."

Several of the Iowa boys grunted their appreciation at the idea and the corporal smiled. "I'll not complain. Sounds like a fine plan to me."

"Well then, relax for a few and enjoy your coffee." He reached into the fire and began to extract the roasted corn, tossing one each to the privates of his detail. He then tossed one to each of the Rebs. Next he pulled the well cooked potatoes from the fire and tossed one to each of his men. Four potatoes remained. "You boys hungry?"

"I don't think the boys would turn it down, smells good enough for us," Corporal Russel said with a smile. He put his brogans back on as he spoke.

"Rebs, catch." Johan tossed the largest potato to the prisoner's fire. Two of them scrambled to catch it. "You Iowa boys have anything to trade, couple-three turnips maybe?"

Corporal Russel nodded. "Fair enough, and if your wife will pass on a loaf of her bread I'll throw in the rest of them."

Johan laughed. "I like turnips. The wife makes a wonderful turnip and salt pork dish that makes me want to thank God I married her."

Corporal Russell leaned back on his knapsack using it as a pillow. "Steele, you've been in a lot of Armies, haven't ya?" He asked as he took off his bummer to wipe the sweat from his brow.

Seth watched Johan consider as he filled his pipe. "I was with the Legion in the Crimea, then joined up with the state of Minnesota at Fort Snelling and re-enlisted again this spring."

"That many years in uniform and not an officer, how do you keep managing that?" Corporal Russell looked like he would honestly like to know. The Sergeant hesitated a moment. Seth hoped he would answer the man seriously. Corporal Russell was an honest Iowa farmer without a rude bone in his body.

Sergeant Steele filled his pipe as he spoke. "I'm still in the Legion, I suppose, but I'm not going back to find out. I have too much self respect to be an officer and they likely would never give a man who cannot read a commission."

Corporal Russell laughed. "You say that, but we both know they've made some pretty big damned fools officers. Either one of us could do twice the job of half those West Point fools!"

"Uncle Billy, Pap Thomas and MacPherson are some of those west Pointers, and I have certainly served under worse. Like that politician McClernand." Johan pulled a smoldering twig from the fire and used it to light his pipe. "I think little of the political men... I guess it shows."

Corporal Russel smiled. "Yeah, but look at Blackjack Logan. He's done fine by us."

"Very true. Logan is a good man. I like him." Sergeant Steele said as he puffed on his pipe. "Not enough Generals like him. Then again, Bragg is a Pointer, he's made a mess of the Rebs for us. Pretty much gave us Missionary Ridge."

"Forrest is one of those who didn't come from the Point."

Sergeant Steele grimaced. "True, but I think Cleburne came up in the British Army..." He turned towards the Rebel prisoners. "Johnny Reb; what do you think of Bragg and Forrest?"

One short but powerful man looked hard at Johan and replied in a thick Southern accent. "Forrest is a scrapper; Bragg couldn't fight his way out of a wet bag. You got another tater?"

Both the Corporal and the Sergeant laughed. Corporal Russel reached into a bag and pulled a large onion from it. He weighed it carefully in his hand and tossed it to the man.

Seth watched the Sergeant consider a moment. "I am happy as a Sergeant. I command at most one hundred men, usually less than a quarter of that. I make certain they are fed and take care of themselves. I need not worry about decisions that can kill hundreds of men. No, I do not envy the officers."

Corporal Russel nodded in agreement. "But I bet you'd like their pay."

But Sergeant Steele shook his head. "I prefer my pride."

Corporal Russel laughed. "I can understand that, I think. Did you boys hear what happened to some cav last week?"

Seth almost laughed as he leaned forward. "Do tell, Corporal."

Corporal Russel leaned back and stretched cracking his fingers against his neck as he did so. "A squad of cav was tracking some Reb guerrillas, probably not unlike these rascals." He sneered as he pointed to the prisoners. "Least ways the cav stopped at some old widows house and they swapped some coffee for some tea." He paused for a moment. "She poisoned them, a whole company! Well, a Reb regiment was waiting for the signal and they charged in to finish them off. Killed every single man. But they missed one, the little negro guide. He hid in the well and then ran and got a big bunch of Wisconsin boys and let me tell you, they got a bit rowdy! Burned the house and whipped the Rebs..." He stopped abruptly as he saw the grins on Seth and Kevin's face. It didn't help that William was burying his head in his hat trying not to laugh out loud.

"What the…"

Sergeant Steele looked at his pipe. "The story has been greatly… what is the word, embellished? It was not a company, but less than a dozen cavalry and it was not a Wisconsin regiment but a Minnesota company; ours. That story is almost as bad as the 'Charge of the Naked Norsemen.'"

"What really happened then, Yank?" The question was not from the Iowa corporal but the short and powerful Rebel who had commented earlier.

All eyes settled on the man; he was what any one of them would have called the average soldier of the Confederacy. He had the build of a man who had marched from here to eternity on half rations, no pay and damned little thanks. A fighting man of the highest order, the kind that you had to respect.

"Were you there Johnny Reb?" Sergeant Steele asked a little testily.

"No, just rid over the field after."

"Seth; you tell the story," the Sergeant said.

Seth thought for a moment, wondering if he too should embellish the story a bit. No, the truth was more than enough. "Well, the Corporal was partly right. There was a troop or so of cav chasing some guerrillas. We were on the same road a couple miles behind them. The guide was our little Sven. He knew the road because he had been up and down it with us a score of times. They stopped at a creek to water their horses and the woman of the local farm came down and gave them some tea. Those cav boys figured that was pretty nice of her and gifted her a poke sack of coffee. Witch had laced the tea with yellow jasmine. Two of the men died and three more got plenty sick.

"The bushwackers come charging out of the woods whooping and hollering. We were close to hand and heard; Captain double-quicked us through the trees and we gave them a volley. Little Foot back tracked them to the old witch's barn.

We emptied her larder and cast her from the house so we could fire the place without her in it. A Reb Captain rode up and demanded we follow the rules of civilized warfare and not make war upon poor widow women. The Sergeant here noted he had a more than passing family resemblance to the old witch and Sven told us he had been at the head of the Reb guerrillas when they charged." Seth chuckled darkly.

"You never saw a man get off a horse so quick. There must have been a score of rifles pointed at his belly. We made the man dig the graves for the two dead cav boys and then another." He paused there and was silent for a moment; even in the dark he knew it was evident he was blushing in shame. "The Sergeant ran him through with his bayonet and then told the old woman her son had paid for her sins."

The Reb spit into his fire. "We got told some of the same when we came up on the place. Old woman was still crying over the grave of her boy. A couple of the wounded you people left there told us the story. You at least could have left them some water."

Sergeant Steele grunted. "We were hoping the dogs would die."

"They are men!" The Reb protested.

"I have killed many a man, but I have never used poison. To poison a man is an evil thing, The kind of thing done by cowards. To die from poison by someone pretending kindness is an evil of old and deserves no sympathy. She knows why her boy died."

Kevin added, "Plus not a one of us in the Company could have put a rope around a woman's neck, no matter how much she might have deserved it."

Johan watched the barn take light and burst into flame; it cast a lurid glow across the sky. He took the pipe from his pocket and absently packed it with tobacco he had taken from the gutted guerrilla that lay dead at his feet.

He could hear Seth praying behind him. It was an appropriate prayer: "If my people, who are called by name, will humble themselves and pray and see my face and turn from their wicked ways, then will I hear from heaven and forgive their sin and will heal their land." His voice carried across the entire yard, and it carried pain within. How could it not?

The Bible was a constant companion to that man. Johan admitted that he while he still did not share that faith, he nevertheless envied it. What was it Seth was so fond of saying? "The Lord gives and the Lord takes away." That was a fact; life was no doubt a bit of amusement for God.

Johan flinched away from the heat as the house erupted into flame. What would Seth say the Lord wanted in this place? Man had intruded his own special brand of hell here.

Perhaps the fire would cleanse it.

The family that had lived here had been against Secession. At least, they said they had been when they came into the garrison wanting to reclaim their ancestral farm.

The local government had confiscated their land and they had been forced to flee north.

Local guerrillas knew them and had come for them in the night. What they had done was not human; not the actions of men, but beasts at best. Johan looked down at the dead guerrilla at his feet and spit on the corpse. Those who dared call the Lakota savages had not seen what men like this could do.

"Sergeant! Just what in the hell have you done?" The Captain's voice cut across the yard.

Johan turned to the Captain. He looked haggard, and as angry as Johan had ever seen him.

"Justice, sir," Johan replied simply.

"What? I didn't order this, I..." He stopped as he saw the dead man at Johan's feet.

"Guerrillas, bandits. They murdered the family and were using the place as a base." He looked back at the burning house and barn.

"What the hell did you hang them for? I will not condone murder, Sergeant!" The Captain was only growing angrier. "I passed those hanged men in the lane. I will not allow you to execute prisoners!"

Johan looked at the Captain. "They were not men."

The Captain exploded in rage. "Like hell! They were Rebel soldiers..."

Johan pinned the Captain with his eyes and raised his hand in a motion for the Captain to quiet himself. "They murdered the family, sir, the whole family."

"What?" The Captain was startled enough to calm down slightly.

"They tortured the father and grandfather and then made them watch as they raped the wife and two little girls," Johan said around his pipe. "Big Josh and his mess buried what was left. Seth just finished speaking over the grave. I hanged those responsible."

"How do you know *these* men did it?" the Captain demanded as he pointed to the grisly fruit at the edge of the lane.

Johan absently kicked the dead guerrilla. "This one talked. I promised not to hang him."

"How did you even know..." the Captain began.

"Little Foot tracked them here; we found the rest," Johan said.

The Captain stared at Johan. "You should have..."

"No, I gave them a soldier's justice," he said coldly.

"You're certain this was the responsible party?" the Captain asked as he looked to the burning buildings.

"Little Foot tracked them," Johan repeated, knowing that was all that need be said.

"I'm not certain what you prefer, the bayonet or the rope..." the Captain mused out loud as if to himself.

Johan was unsure if an answer was needed, but he answered anyway. "Bayonet. You look into the eyes of the man as you kill him. It is close and it is personal. The rope is reserved for those who deserve nothing more."

Seth sat on his bunk letting his legs dangle and looked at his shaking hands. It wasn't cold but he couldn't make his hands stop trembling. Sebastian and Little Josh were playing a game of chuck a luck but they weren't betting, just taking turns throwing the dice. The barracks held a sullen silence, the normal jokes and bawdy stories missing. They had killed men today; some might even accuse them of murder. No man here tonight would though. Sergeant Steele called it soldier's justice, and not a man here would disagree with that. God's justice had been done and he had been part of it, an instrument of His justice.

Unable to turn away, Seth had watched the executions. The men had danced upon the end of the ropes in a futile last grasp at life. Once he knew they were dead, he had prayed over the victims of those animals. He was not sorry. The only guilt he felt was the inability to protect those who had been so brutally treated. He was a soldier protecting the innocent and weak.

It was what he was supposed to do.

He had always told his sister everything... but this? How could he describe such a thing? She didn't deserve to know of such evil.

They had been on one of the Colonel's patrols. Sergeant Steele didn't believe in slow or easy paced patrols. If the orders called for a five mile patrol the Sergeant was guaranteed to add at least an extra mile, usually two or three. His patrols never quite followed the expected path or road, though but you could usually see the road from wherever they were.

If the opportunity arose, Little Foot came along; always alone, just off on one flank or the other. That's how the old wagon road and the tracks of the bushwackers had been found. William had asked how the Sergeant knew they were bushwackers.

"Cavalry puts out vedettes, farmers ride mules and pull a wagon." He was right.

Seth thought he had seen the demon of war on the fields of battle; he knew now he had been wrong. They had not been men but animals... no, they were monsters. What they had done was beyond the pale. The evidence they left of their activities created a cold pit in the souls of the men that no amount of prayer or whiskey could ever wash away. They left scars, as the war itself had never done.

The victims of the guerrillas had been real people. They could have been his own family, or that of any man in the company. Seth shuddered at the thought of Carlie or his mother at the hands of such monsters. Until today, stories of atrocities against the innocent had been just that, stories. But the reality of the worst that mankind could visit upon one another had been shown to them and they could never again deny it. They had seen evil today; a kind of evil they would never even attribute to the most savage Indian. It had hardened their hearts to the point that a guerrilla or bushwacker held little chance of survival if facing them.

They had hanged them, all except one. Sergeant Steele had gutted him and left him to die a slow and agonizing death. Not one man felt guilty or ashamed of the Sergeant's actions. It was justice, the justice of a soldier.

Allatoona
October, 1864

The Battle of Allatoona Pass on October 5th, 1864, is often referred to as the bloodiest battle of the Civil War, with 30% casualties in less than four hours... a little less than five casualties per minute.

$\mathfrak{J}$ohan looked at the train on the siding and grimaced as he saw the stewards dumping slops, dirty bandages and other refuse onto the grass. The cars were full of wounded men destined for hospitals further north.

It had rained all last night and well into the morning; that would spare these men some of the heat at least. There were still scores of large puddles about, eerily reflecting torch and lamplight. The engine quietly puffed smoke as it built steam and readied to move, adding darkness to the night. Sebastian, Bryce, Emmanuel and Nate lay on the slope below him catching a few minutes of rest. The rest of the mess was long abed, or should have been. He half suspected Seth was still awake writing another one of his letters to his sister or that woman of Kyrie's, Maxine.

Johan marveled a moment as he thought of Seth. How he had managed to arrange Maxine's passage north he could not figure. Johan suspected Mina and maybe a few members of the mess had helped with that. But it had been a good idea to bring her to Minnesota when the regiment had been on furlough. It was important that Emaline and Sven have a place away from the war, and putting Maxine in charge of those two children was a stroke of genius that Johan would not have thought of. Maxine might have been a whore in Vicksburg but she was well educated and a far cry from a fool. Johan rather suspected she had initiated her friendship with Seth in order to gain a husband that might send her away from the war and to a new beginning where none knew her soiled past. What a woman might do to survive in war... well, he would not judge her for that as most would. In Minnesota she would have that chance at a fresh beginning. But Seth was no fool. Johan was fairly certain the boy held no illusions toward Maxine and he doubted that there was any romance between the two. Instead Seth was doing what he called his Christian duty; likely, the woman would never appreciate it.

Johan was glad Emaline was stayed north. She was a bit of trouble the regiment could do without. Too pretty, and too prone to flights of fancy to allow near so many hungry men. Both William and Sebastian had been sweet on her and the only thing that had prevented bad blood between the two men was their tight friendship. As it was, they had nearly been at each other's throats over the girl. Johan knew Emaline had been interested in one of the men in Webb's mess as well. To make matters worse, he was sure Sven had been a touch in love with her too.

Putting Maxine and Emaline under the care of Carlie had been a wise move, too. Carlie would keep them out of trouble, and her status in the community gave the two women enough legitimacy to keep them from becoming social pariahs. Sven might have managed as a good chaperone for the ladies, but now Carlie would have to do, as Sven had once again managed to make his way back to the regiment.

Sven was a good kid. Johan had no doubt Mina would have adopted him given the chance. But a regiment at war was no place for a child. Though young Sven was a man in mind and heart, his body did not match. Still, his return to the Regiment was welcome. That said, the Captain had made it clear to all that Sven was to go home with the next group of men who mustered out. Johan wondered if the Captain had made it clear to Sven as well. Otherwise, the boy would be back again.

Sebastian and Bryce had spent a good bit of the night loading barrels of fresh water onto the cars while Emmanuel and Nate had distributed baskets full of Mina's fresh bread. Johan was glad that none of his men had been in that train. The fighting on the line must have been ferocious if the casualties were any indication.

These men had been in hospital for a long while before being sent away from Atlanta. Dysentery and fevers afflicted fully as many on this train as lead did. Most were too sick or too badly wounded to move on their own. There were milkmen without jaws or cheeks, and amputees missing arms or legs, but that kind of wounded was the minority. Many were the slow-dying; too tough or stubborn to succumb quickly to a shattered body. Some of these men had been wounded in the heavy fighting of July and August outside of Atlanta, and had been languishing in pain ever since, only just able to be moved now, better than a month and a half later.

Johan hoped that when the time came for the Angel of Death to take him, she would take him quickly. He never wanted to be on one of those trains, wracked by the agony brought by every bump on the track and every lurch of the car. That kind of pain, with the only hope of an end to the pain being death... He shuddered at the thought. Oh, yes. A quick bullet to the head, a visit from the beautiful Angel of Death. Definitely preferable to a trip on a hospital train.

"Sergeant!" The voice was a weary one; the Captain had spent a good part of the evening praying with the wounded men on that last train. He might have been a Captain of the infantry but in his heart he was still a man of God.

Johan snapped to attention. "Yes, sir."

"I want you to take your mess and set to behind the works. Pitch your tents if you like, but I want your boys on hand all night in case they try something sneaky. Two companies are in the rifle pits, but I want you and Sergeant Webb ready in the works. Make certain your men have full canteens and cartridge boxes. While you're at it, have them

206

fill their haversacks with rations." The Captain rubbed his bloodshot eyes and yawned. "Word about is that we might have a problem with Hood; French is headed our way. I want your men ready, in case they come in the night."

"Yes, sir." French... mostly Mississippi men, if he remembered right. At least they wouldn't be Cleburne's men.

"Steele, they're coming. They hit Big Shanty, Moon Station and Acworth... We all know General Sherman needs the rations in the warehouses, but Hood wants them too. We'll have help, but Hood wants this place. We'll catch hell if they don't get here before French. I'm going to tell the First Sergeant too, and then catch an hour or two of sleep." The Captain really looked exhausted and the prospect of this coming battle weighed heavily on him.

"Sir, you get some rest. I will let the First Sergeant know."

The Captain smiled as he looked at Johan. "No, Sergeant, that's my job... but thank you. You're a good Sergeant and a good man."

A good man; it was a compliment that Johan liked and not the kind of thing he had often heard in reference to himself.

He shook his head as he watched the Captain walk towards the quarters of the First Sergeant. French and the Rebel army coming here really only made sense. The only way Hood could hurt Sherman was to harass him by seizing isolated garrisons and supply depots. Hood had learned his lesson hard outside of Atlanta, and it had been a brutal one.

Johan felt the grip of fear in his belly. The garrison here was isolated, not all that large. There was only a single six gun battery and a short brigade of infantry. It was a good place to defend, with two strong forts, but the forts had been built with a larger garrison in mind. And even larger garrisons, with better positions at their backs, had surrendered.

The story of Fort Pillow was well known; the fate of the black soldiers and of their camp followers grew more harrowing and grotesque with each telling. The very thought of Mina at the hands of Rebel soldiers sent a shiver up his spine. Better that she die.

No, men always thought it better that the woman should die. He smiled slightly and wondered if anyone thought to ask the women what they thought of that.

Johan considered for a second. Fear before a battle had never really bothered him after Ischeriden, but this was different. Now he feared losing Mina. Even just being separated from her was not to be tolerated. Death he did not fear. But the idea of being without the only woman who had ever cared for him, the only woman he had ever loved, was a living Hell.

Johan turned and watched the hospital train sputter off into the night. He almost wished he had put Mina on that train. But what kind of life might she make for herself in Chattanooga or Nashville? And would he be able to live without her?

Johan went to get the men of his mess. It was going to be a hard day, he could feel it in his bones. He absently scratched the scar on his neck. They were most of a thousand men and six guns against French and his division, probably the better part of five thousand men. True, the men here were almost all veterans of places like Iuka, Corinth and the Vicksburg campaign, but French commanded men every bit as tough.

Mina looked across the room at her man. It was almost chill, though nothing like a winter eve in Minnesota. The little wood stove the men had given her and Elissa made the shack snug and comfortable. It was as late as she had been awake in many months; well after midnight and she was tired clean through to her bones. Deelia and Marie, with Sven in sullen attendance, had offered to accompany the trainload of casualties to Chattanooga. The stewards hadn't thought twice before they accepted. It had been a long day with laundry and then making bread. Elissa was asleep behind her blanket partition. Mina envied the girl, she received a letter from her family every mail call.

Johan looked nervous, perhaps a bit frightened. It was not something she was used to seeing. He was always so steady. Unshakeable. She knew the Rebels would come and there would be a bad fight. If Johan and the regiment lost the battle, her fate would be a return to slavery or worse. She held no illusions; she was not a white woman and even passing as a halfbreed would spare her nothing. She had heard of the fate of laundresses at Fort Pillow, and it didn't matter if the stories were true or not, or that some of the less likeable men in the regiment had made a point of telling the stories where they knew she could overhear when Johan was not present.

Mina set her jaw and made a decision. If the works fell and men came for her and Elissa, she still had the Colt revolving shotgun Johan had bought for her before they went to trade with the Lakota. She could kill at least two, and if the time came there was enough powder to spare either her or Elissa the horror the soldiers might visit upon them.

"When will they come?" she quietly asked Johan.

"On the morrow. At dawn, most likely." Johan said, just as low-voiced. Mina felt her stomach tighten at his expression, the tension in his body. What did he know, that she didn't?

"Will we hold?" Mina asked even as she feared she already knew the answer.

He stopped filling his haversack with hardtack and looked to her. A look of resolve crossed his face as though he had decided something. "Or I will die in the attempt."

Suddenly Mina realized the cause of his fear. "I will be here waiting for you. The ladies and I will make doughnuts and bring them to the men with buckets of fresh water."

He reached out and took her chin, raising her face so that he could look into her eyes. "No. Stay here, stay safe for me. If they come over the walls, stay in the hospital with Doc Jim and tell them you are the wife of an officer." There was something in his eyes; the fire she had seen before. His fear had passed. Or, he had decided not to let it infect her.

"The bread and water will…"

Johan interrupted. "*No*. If they come over the walls they won't see skirts, they will just shoot. I want you alive. I need you."

Mina smiled slyly; "I know."

A train whistle punctured the silence like a knife. With the sound of that whistle Johan's eyes brightened and he grinned broadly. "That will even the odds some."

"What?" Mina asked, not understanding.

"That would be help, a trainload of soldiers. Another thousand men, maybe." He grinned suddenly. "Tomorrow will be a bad day for French and his men."

"Do you remember Mrs. Barnaby asked you to watch over Seth…"

Johan interrupted her again. "I know. I'm putting him below the head log loading for us. I promised I would do what I could, but when they come over the wall he will face the same danger as all of us."

210

Johan stepped close and wrapped his arms around her in a gentle hug. She heard him inhale the scent of her hair and she hugged him back.

"I love you, Johan. You stay alive for me."

She almost heard him grin as he kissed her forehead. "I will do as I can."

The man she loved picked up his rifle and stepped into the darkness.

It was well after dawn, sometime after ten in the morning and they had not come in a full-on attack yet. There had been only skirmishing so far. Seth smiled to himself. Back home he would have finished the morning chores and be just thinking about dinner.

He could see the Rebs in the distance. They had been skirmishing with the outposts for a couple hours. But now it was silent, no firing anywhere. It was amazing how a flag of truce, really nothing more than a scrap of bed sheet, could silence a field of battle. There would be a battle today, once the truce had run its course. None had any doubt of that. They all knew Sergeant Steele to be right when he had told them so, and a half-dozen Rebel flags only drove that point home.

They had heard the rumors about Hood being at Big Shanty. All had been worried, but then the train had arrived with General Corse and part of his brigade. They were men from Illinois and an Iowa regiment, veterans all. They had doubled the size of the garrison and injected some much needed confidence in all of the men.

First the Captain had them fall to in the Eastern fort, then when Corse and his beautiful men had shown up, the Captain had them act as guides to Corse's men and they'd fallen in with a gun crew from the 12th Wisconsin Battery for the fight. It was clear this was where the first blow would fall.

He could see the flag of truce leaving the works. Those were held by the 93rd Illinois; the 39th Iowa and 7th Illinois with that big Napoleon square in the center. Their half company was just icing on the cake. The Rebel officer carrying the flag wasn't thirty feet from him; Seth had an odd urge to ask him if they could just settle this over a game of chuck-a-luck.

The Rebs were done with their parley. All here knew the mind of General Corse: "Hold at all hazards; help is on the way." Some Rebel sharpshooters were moving up closer to the works; there was a depression there and from their side it must have looked like a better protected way to get at the garrison. They didn't know the thick abattis blocked any advantage in either field of fire or movement. There was a brigade of infantry behind them, close enough for a quick dash. But the boys with that big Napoleon could hold that spot of the works as long as their ammunition held out.

Seth looked at the rest of the mess; all men he knew and trusted, good solid men to have beside you in a fight. Kevin and William had come to be tight friends. Bryce and Joshua were as good solid fighters as you could want beside you in a fight. Nate and Emmanuel were so alike they had a tendency to finish each other sentences, and there was little doubt that Nate idolized the older Emmanuel. It was fitting that they were *copains*. Then there was the big monster Sebastian; Seth loved that man like a brother and hoped to introduce him to Carlie after the war. Sebastian would make a wonderful brother-in-law.

The mess was led by Sergeant Steele. Seth hadn't called him Johan in three years. It didn't matter that others addressed him by his first name, it just didn't seem right to him. Sometimes Seth hated the man with his whole being, but most of the time he had come to view the older man as an older brother.

Actually, no, that wasn't quite right. If he was totally honest, he had to admit that he looked to Johan as a father figure.

Most of the company was in this section of the works on either side of the gun sandwiched between the 39th Iowa and the 7th Illinois with men from the 93rd Illinois spread throughout as they fell back from the rifle pits. Sergeant Webb's mess was down to about six men with the toughest man being the Dakota Little Foot. Big Josh's mess was full of good men that Seth enjoyed sharing chapel with. There was the Captain with a box of cartridges. The war had thinned him to a skeleton of the man they had elected as their officer back in '61. He had refused two promotions to "stay with his flock" and the men all loved him for it. There were barely fifty men left in the company, less than half who had signed the roster in Fort Snelling. Disease and the war had claimed so many…

Seth knew more would fall today. Perhaps even all of them.

The sudden Rebel yell to the west snapped his head around to see a sizeable Reb force not two hundred yards away charging the works. They were greeted almost immediately by a crashing volley that slowed them, followed by the roar of that big gun firing a load of canister, which tore an ugly swath through them. Then another part of the works took up the firing and any thoughts of peace were gone. God, but it was inspiring and terrible at the same time.

"Angels and ministers of grace preserve us." Seth said quietly.

"Remember what they did to us at Vicksburg? It's our turn." Kevin shouted as he sighted down his rifle and sent a round towards the mass of rebels.

Seth watched the attack develop like a cascading wall of water. The works were enveloped in the roar of musketry and cannon fire as two of the battery's ordnance rifles in the Star Fort lobbed shells into the faces of the attackers. Those Wisconsin gunners knew their job and added their voices to the crescendo of battle with chilling effect. In a way it was beautiful watching man measuring man; and terrifying as well.

"Seth and Josh, load for William and Kevin; Nate and Sebastian, for Bryce and Emmanuel. They come for us." Though not shouting, Sergeant Steele was loud enough to be heard over the din of battle.

The roar of battle increased and Seth turned to look towards the 39th. The Rebels were coming at them along-side the Alabama Road. It looked to be intense fighting with a good bit of it hand to hand already. The Rebs were pushing and making those Iowa boys move.

"HERE THEY COME!!!" Sergeant Boraas shouted the warning and all eyes took in the sight of the first line of Rebs pouring out of the cannon smoke not ten paces from the works. With a pull of the lanyard the gun erupted in a roar; the recoil lifting the wheels off of the ground. It had been double-shotted with canister... good Lord. Seth looked under the headlog and saw nothing but smoke and blood where a moment ago thirty men had stood.

Seth turned to look and saw them coming from the north as well; there were at least two Regiments climbing that steep hillside, maybe more. It was most of sixty feet up in less than a hundred yards. He felt his guts knot. If they were coming up that way with the men on the other side of the railroad cut shooting into their flank, there was no stopping them. A hand on his shoulder pushed him down below the firing step and away from the head log.

"Look at that." Sergeant Steele said, wonder in his voice as he pointed to a sergeant calmly carrying a chair across the field to their rear. A rebel cannon ball hit half a dozen paces behind him and bounced high into the air disappearing off to the north. The Sergeant didn't even flinch as he moved. Not a care in the world as he carried a chair into the works! The insanity of it clearly amused Sergeant Steele because he laughed as he turned back towards the enemy.

Sergeant Steele was still chuckling as he spoke. "Stay off the firing step; I want you loading." There was something different about the Sergeant this morning. A different look in the eye; the coldness was gone or well hidden.

Seth handed his loaded rifle to William and started the process of loading an empty one. William was firing as fast as he could while Kevin picked his targets more carefully. The Sergeant fired only occasionally, doing his best to make every round count.

It had been only a few minutes. The volume of fire and canister from the works savaged the assault, tearing huge gaps in the lines. It wasn't the first time French's men learned that westerners could shoot straight. Probably wouldn't be the last time either.

"Kevin, Emmanuel, aim for officers and anything with a chevron on the sleeves." The Sergeant was back to his normal cold self. "If they come over, use your bayonets. And make no mistake, they will get over. But they must not pass. Do you all understand?" Steele looked into the eyes of every man in the mess as he gave his order; there was no doubting his will. Seth smiled as he realized that every man agreed with him. This hill was theirs, and by the will of the Good Lord they were going to hold it.

A piercing war cry that could only belong to Little Foot turned every head to the mess of Sergeant Webb. Bryan was down with a hole through his head and Sergeant Webb was writhing on the ground with a shattered shoulder. Dave and Glenn had stepped up onto the firing step and were sending rounds down range with great enthusiasm. Little Foot had his war paint on and was chanting his queer war song.

"It is a death song. He plans to die today." Sergeant Steele spoke to no one in particular. Seth had no idea how the Sergeant knew that and he really didn't care at the moment. He just shook his head at the insanity of it. If French's men had their way, the Dakota man might just get his wish.

"How many times will they come?" Seth asked.

"Until they know there is no hope of taking this place."

The fire increased to a crescendo as the Rebels closed on the abattis. "They're aiming for us!" William shouted.

Seth felt his stomach clench; they might come over the wall at any second. Nate looked at him and they shared a nervous grin. Josh handed a loaded rifle to Bryce and watched blood spray from the man's shoulder. Bryce let out a yell of pain and stepped back from the head log. A round had cut a groove across his shoulder; it was a bloody wound but not crippling. The language coming from Bryce made Nate drop his jaw in shock, and Seth blushed.

"Nice! I will have to remember that one!" Sergeant Steele said with a smile.

Nate stepped up to the firing step and snapped a shot into the faces of the advancing rebels. "They ain't falling back."

"Learn how to shoot, you gutless sheep! Your mothers were cheap Biloxi whores and your fathers were goats!" Steele laughed as a score of rounds smacked into the head log over his head in reply to his loud taunt. "My, my, they think I am a touch irritating!"

"I can't imagine why, Sergeant; you are such a charming..." Nate was interrupted as a well aimed, or lucky, minnie smashed against his temple.

Emmanuel caught him as he fell. Seth and anyone else who looked could see the wound was fatal.

"NO!!!!!" Emmanuel screamed; rage and anguish showing themselves on his face. Only Seth heard his next words, as he gently laid Nate's body on the ground behind the firing step. "He only came to look after me..." For just a moment in the chaos of battle, Emmanuel stared silently at his friend. Then as Seth watched, the expression on his face changed, becoming harder, colder, less anguished. "Goddamn sons of bitches," Nate's *copain* whispered... then screamed, "YOU GODDAMN SONS OF BITCHES!" He grabbed up his rifle and sent a snap shot into the teeth of the advancing Confederates. "I'm gonna kill every last one of you bastards." And Seth shuddered, knowing Emmanuel's words weren't so much a curse as a wrathful promise.

"HERE THEY COME!!" Sergeant Boraas yelled again. At his words a sheet of fire left the works as the rebels came on.

Seth burned his hand on the hot barrel of William's rifle. He looked up at the head log as a Rebel soldier emerged over the top. William shot him at such close range that

217

the muzzle flash ignited the Rebel soldier's jacket. Others showed themselves and Seth watched as Sergeant Steele almost touched his rifle to a man before he fired.

In the blink of an eye the Sergeant had fixed his bayonet and was sparring with a big Rebel in a ragged shell jacket. In moments the Rebel fell with his throat ripped open.

A score of Rebels erupted over the head log. Bryce was there fighting like a lion, his rifle swinging to and fro like a massive club. Out of the corner of his eye he saw Little Foot leap into the fray, screaming like the wild Indian he was.

The Rebels exploded into the works like an inexorable wave. Seth swung the butt of his rifle at a rebel and missed. The man's face was contorted into a horrid grimace and he laughed like a demon as he thrust his bayonet at Seth's face. Seth knew he was going to die. Everything moved so slowly, like a bad dream. There was no way he could avoid the bayonet plunging toward his throat, but still he tried to dodge away from it...

The steel of the bayonet on the end of Sergeant Steele's rifle caught the Rebel bayonet with the ringing clang of steel on steel and the Rebel's bayonet only grazed Seth's throat. He felt the sting of the blade as it split skin.

Sergeant Steele stepped into the man, deftly pushing away the bayonet with his own blade as he did so then he smashed the Rebel's face with a short and vicious jab from his rifle butt, transforming the man's visage into a geyser of blood. With a quick reverse of his rifle, the Sergeant drove his bayonet into the man's belly and with a vicious slap of the stock disemboweled him. A man's life ended in the blink of an eye.

Johan turned and smiled an evil grin at Seth; "Kill or die, you fool." For the first time Seth truly understood the value of all of that bayonet drill.

The fighting was all hand to hand now, an insane fury of men fighting for their lives. Bayonets, clubbed muskets, fists and even teeth were all used to effect. One Rebel officer was throwing clods of clay, and Seth felt one bounce off his head. Off to his right, he saw the Captain shatter a man's skull with an empty cartridge crate and Emmanuel was everywhere, screaming with the high pitched voice of a banshee. There was Sergeant Steele using his bayonet as an introduction to the Angel of Death he spoke of so often. Sergeant Steele was an artist, a killer who visited death upon those he could reach and he had saved Seth's life.

Then it was over as quick as a blink, no more Rebels fighting them. Perhaps two score had made it over the works, and those that remained lay dead or wounded on the ground. Bryce lay below the fire step, now grievously wounded, his shattered and bloody rifle still tightly gripped in his hand. Emmanuel was also injured, with a jagged wound above his right eye and tears of rage and hate coursing down his blood-smeared cheek. No less than three rebels lay dead at his feet. Sebastian lay dead with a crushed skull and Joshua was puking his guts out next to Sebastian's corpse. Blood poured from a vicious head wound and he was also apparently the victim of a strong blow to the stomach.

The drummer boy, Blair, was suddenly there with a quickly improvised travois; he dragged Bryce and Joshua back towards the Star Fort and safety, and tried to do the same with Emmanuel.

"No, I'm going to send some more of them on to hell where they belong." Blood dripped down his face onto his hands and jacket.

"Get the gun! Get it back to the Star Fort!" the Captain bellowed.

Emmanuel laughed the harsh cackle of a witch. "Come to me so that I might kill you!" he snarled as he fired into the face of a man trying to climb over the works.

Seth touched the burning wound at his throat. A half inch in either direction and he would be looking into the beautiful eyes of the Angel of Death that Sergeant Steele spoke of so often, and awaiting the judgment of the good Lord. He owed the man his life. He loaded the rifle William handed him as quickly as possible. The acrid smell of gun smoke and taste of sulphur dominated his senses. The blood from his throat wound combined with sweat to make his hands slick and sticky enough to make loading difficult. He felt his hand unconsciously rub the wound at his throat… the sweat and powder on his hand made the wound burn.

"Barnaby, help move the goddamned gun!" the Captain screamed at him. "Right now!"

God, he missed his sister and the farm. He would give his very soul to be home working with the horses. He flinched as a round whistled past his head. He turned to see his friends fighting for their lives at the wall.

"*Move*, damn it!" one of the artillery noncoms demanded and gave a hollow cry as a bullet smashed him to the ground.

"*MERDE!*" Seth heard Sergeant Steele curse loudly from behind him, then roar, "YOU UGLY ENGLISH WHORES! YOUR MOTHERS WERE SHEEP AND FATHERS DRUNKEN DOGS!"

Seth turned to look at Sergeant Steele; he was fine, back to his normal self. And the rest of his friends were there beside him, covering the withdrawal of the big Napoleon.

Seth could see Sebastian's and Nate's crumpled bodies. He said a silent prayer for them as he went back to the task of helping move that cursed heavy gun up the slope to the Star Fort.

It wasn't much more than a couple hundred yards, but it seemed like miles. As they rolled the gun into the fort and set it in position Seth looked at the carnage around the western works and the stream of men in blue racing for the protection of the Star Fort. How many of his friends were out there dead? Sebastian and Nate, who else? Even those few were too many.

Kevin chose that moment to hold out his Springfield for him to take and Seth stared at it a moment.

"Load it yourself, Kevin, I've got this to do." Seth said as he stepped onto the firing step and searched for a target with his own rifle. They were just squirrels and rabbits, like hunting back home.

Kevin grunted his approval and began the process of loading.

Sergeant Steele and Emmanuel appeared beside him.

Seth sighted down the barrel of his rifle, picking a target. He didn't know if he'd ever killed a man before. Three years, and as far as he knew a man had never fallen to his rifle. He had fired into the enemy line many a time, but this was different. They were so close you could see their faces and there was little doubt where the bullet went.

But these were squirrels. They were just squirrels. Their uniforms were gray or butternut brown like the hide of a squirrel. And like a squirrel, when one fell another popped up to replace it. Not like men at all. They were squirrels.

The scene outside the fort was one from hell; smoke and death everywhere. He sighted on a color bearer, then shifted his aim to a sword-waving officer beside the man and squeezed the trigger. He didn't hear the weapon fire as the ordnance rifle in the embrasure let go with double canister. It struck at the feet of the front rank and cut a hideous swath from the front to the back of the charging rebel column. The whole road turned crimson with the blood of the dead and dying, and the scene imprinted on his mind.

Seth stepped down from the firing step and began loading again. A few seconds later he stepped up to look under the head log for a new target; the last of the Rebels were filing into whatever cover they could find. It wouldn't take long for them to reform and come again. Seth looked around the fort and saw men from several regiments working together. There was a man with one of those Henry rifles sending rounds into the faces of the enemy just as fast as he could work the lever. It was terrifying to see. He couldn't imagine what it was like on the other side of the line.

"HERE THEY COME!!!" Sergeant Boraas shouted again. A quick look at Boraas's mess showed no men down and they'd made it safely into the fort. They had lost Tyler and Luke at Vicksburg and Gavin, Richard and Steve were lost before that during the Iuka campaign. The five men that were left would hold their section as well as any. He watched them volley into the advancing Rebels as he turned to give the squirrels another bullet.

Sergeant Steele slapped him on the shoulder. "Pay no mind to anything but what is in front of you. Kill them or they will kill you. Next time you are looking at the wrong end of a weapon it might be that nobody will be able to help you." His powder streaked face and blood covered weapon and hands made him look like a demon from the depths of hell itself. Then, too, although the Sergeant was a sight to frighten Rebels and small children, his very presence was in a way reassuring to Seth.

It went on forever. They kept coming trying to climb the steep slope of the fort to get at them and they fell by the score. The barrels of the men's weapons grew so hot they could no longer load them. One man was standing by the burning cotton bales at the sally port urinating into the barrel of his weapon. Not exactly the way the manual described for cleaning, but it probably worked well enough. The ammunition for the cannon was all gone, Fullington from the battery had already been back and forth across the bridge three times to keep the three guns supplied with ammunition. The kind of courage it took to brave that run was hard to imagine.

Everyone but the rest of the regiment and a few companies of the 18th Wisconsin were in the Star Fort. They were three to four men deep at the fire steps; with the best shot forward and rest to load, they put out a wall of fire that was all but insurmountable.

Seth and Kevin were side by side shooting as fast as they could pick a target and there were plenty of targets. The cotton bales that had been used to block the sally port were on fire, adding stinging smoke and heat to the hell inside the earthen walls of the fort. Dead and wounded men were just pushed into the center of the fort to suffer,. No more could be done. The center of the fort was a scene from the very depths of hell.

"Squirrels, just squirrels…" Seth said to himself over and over again.

Johan looked at the carnage strewn about the western works and around the Star Fort. There were hundreds of bodies; whether clad in blue, gray, or butternut no longer mattered, they were equal in death. Many still writhed in the anguish of horrid wounds. Pitiful voices weakly begging for water or their mothers; others begged for an end to the pain. Johan looked down at his own gore covered bayonet. The blood had dried to a thick heavy crust. Hard to believe that not long ago it had been the lifeblood that coursed through the hearts of men.

He knelt down and plunged the blade into the earth a few times, then wiped what remained off on the jacket of a dead Rebel. Just one more upon the butcher's bill, young and with features that in an odd way resembled those of Seth. This young man had died in agony, visibly wracked in pain with his eyes staring into the sky and his fingers dug into the earth as though trying to hold his spirit in his body. Johan reached down and closed the man's eyes, then riffled his pockets; a letter and a picture. The eyes of a pretty girl of maybe fifteen looked back at him. He carefully put them both back into the man's pocket and stood up.

He looked at the Star Fort. The bodies in the center of the fort were being removed and laid out in preparation for burial. They had died hard, as soldiers were wont to do. Blue lay beside butternut, all so young, and the true tragedy was that they were all Americans.

Johan looked about for the form of Mina. She was still helping at the hospital, but he could see her carrying a bucket of water from the well. She wore her blue dress, the one he had bought her in Charleston. It was showing its age and even from the better part of a hundred yards he could see the blood spattered across the front of her apron. The surgeons were gladly availing themselves of her assistance and he was rather certain other laundresses were there too. The hospital was full of men from both sides of the argument and he had no doubt the Angel of Death was far from finished with her work.

French's men had managed to push them back into the Star Fort and had likely captured some men as well, but those Henrys and Springfields along with the cannon had made them pay a steep price for attacking Allatoona. Yet the butcher's bill was in no way worth the prize. If French's losses were much less than a thousand men Johan would have been surprised. The garrison and their reinforcements had paid a bloody price as well. Though no regiment got off without loss, the 39th Iowa was a wreck and when combined with the 7th Illinois they had to have lost three hundred men between them. All told, probably no less than five hundred men of the garrison killed and wounded in less than four hours of hell. Johan shook his head as he tried to compare it to the assaults on Vicksburg or Sevastopol. It just seemed so different.

The still body of Sergeant Webb, killed as he was being carried back to the Star Fort, lay beside a Rebel officer that was barely of an age to shave. A bullet had struck the young officer above the right temple. Johan wondered if that was a bit of his work, or of another man. It bothered him little that he had killed men; he had done so many times before. Only the new recruits or those with a gentle soul seemed to have a problem with the gore and death strewn about them. The rest of the men were veterans who had seen their share and become jaded to the horror of it.

His gaze fell upon Little Foot, who was naked to the waist and covered in powder and gore. The young Dakota was calmly relieving another dead Rebel officer of his scalp. He tore loose the scalp and raised it to the sky with a blood curdling scream of triumph. Four more fresh scalps hung from the sling on his cartridge box.

It was one thing to relieve the dead of their money and gear, but mutilating them was too much even for Johan. Johan knew Sergeant Webb had stopped Little Foot from mutilating bodies after Corinth. But Webb was gone now. Johan had won real money on the Dakota boy when he ran foot races and liked him all the more for it. He was honest and loyal to his friends; a good man. He would ask the Captain to put Little Foot in his mess. At least he knew the man's language.

"Little Foot, put those out of sight. The Captain will not approve." Johan knew his Lakota was rusty and was probably not quite spoken correctly, but he knew the Captain would not understand what was said and that Little Foot would. Little Foot's dark eyes looked into his a moment, then he nodded his head and tucked the scalps behind his cartridge box.

Neck and face blood-streaked and filthy, Emmanuel finished dragging another dead Rebel to the foot of Nate's corpse, "placing the dogs where they belonged," as he put it. Seth was doing what he could to prepare the body of Sebastian for shipment home, hands working gently. All the while, the new little cat Sebastian had claimed sat and cried upon his still chest. Johan hoped the laundresses would adopt the creature. He smiled at that thought; imagine worrying about a lost cat amidst so much carnage. Johan's mess was not the only one about hard work as men cared for their friends and comrades' shattered and broken bodies.

Joshua would be lucky to survive his injuries. Though not bloody, Johan knew his insides were at the very least severely bruised. Bryce was at hospital too, badly wounded in several places. Emmanuel would need several days in hospital as well, though he would not go there until he had set his friend Nate for burial. He was forever a changed man; the death of his *copain* had cracked his mind. It was plain in his voice and manner, and his eyes were dead now. Johan had seen it before. Emmanuel would never be the same again, and men would suffer for his pain.

Johan looked to Sergeant Boraas' mess. Only a couple of his men had been wounded, and then only lightly. One had to admire the big Sergeant. He kept good rein upon his men, and few had suffered badly in the war. Though not a practiced soldier when the war had begun, he had learned quickly and in most ways Sergeant Boraas was a better man than he, and Johan knew it.

Webb's mess had all but ceased to exist. Only Little Foot had passed the fight without a severe wound, and that was certainly not for lack of trying; the man had been in the thick of the fighting, literally jumping in with knife in hand. Christ, but these were hard men, and Johan was proud to stand beside them.

General Order 86, October 7, 1864

The general commanding avails himself of this opportunity, in the handsome defense made of Allatoona, to illustrate the most important principle in war, that fortified places should be defended to the last, regardless of the relative numbers of the party attacking and attacked... The thanks of this army are due and are hereby accorded to General Corse, Colonel Tourtellotte, Colonel Rowett, officers and men, for their determined and gallant defense of Allatoona, and it is made an example to illustrate the importance of preparing in time, and meeting the danger, when present, boldly, manfully, and well.

Commanders and garrisons of the posts along our railroads are hereby instructed that they must hold their posts to the last minute, sure that the time gained is valuable and necessary to their comrades at the front.

By order of Major General W.T. Sherman.

To the Sea, an End

Sherman's March to the Sea broke the back of the Confederacy. It proved to the world that the Confederacy was a hollow shell. The scars of that March remain still in the bitterness and hate shown toward the men who shattered that facade.

ohan looked at the battery of guns parked alongside the road as he and the rest of the column marched by. They were resting their horses in a stand of pines, and a few of the men were making coffee over a hastily built fire. The coffee smelled good.

The guns had seen hard use and showed it, and so did the men. There was no spit and polish on the part of this battery. In no way were they pretty and ready for inspection by some martinet officer.

Johan knew the reputation of these men and their guns; their flag bore battle honors from such places as Shiloh, Iuka, Corinth and a score of other tough battles on their way to Atlanta. The rumor was about that they had lost and regained two guns during the big battle for Atlanta. They had also lost more than half of their horses and about a quarter of the men. He didn't doubt the truth of it, as he could see the distinctive file marks around touchholes on two of the guns. They had been spiked at some point, and one did not spike guns unless things were very hot indeed.

Johan grinned as he recalled the competition this battery and one fresh from the Army of the Potomac had had in the spring. Each battery had three shots at a fence post a thousand yards distant. That other battery sure had looked pretty, every bit of brass polished to a mirror sheen. They had done well in the competition, getting one round within six feet of the fence post. *This* battery had squarely shattered that post with their second bolt. The westerners had watched the button polishers fire and adjusted their own fire to nail the target. Was it any wonder the Rebs had such respect for Union guns?

They were the equal of any in the old world, the kind of battery he wanted supporting him in battle. It was not important how they looked, so long as they stood and fought. Johan turned to review the men of his company. They were as tough as any he had ever served beside. They moved at that long swinging gait distinctive to this army; the steady tramp of thousands of tough fighting men used to the march. He considered a moment. Only his *copain* Remi and the Swiss corporal that had gifted him his pipe were half the marksman of even a third of the men in this company. He was willing to wager that a good number of the men in this company could put a ball into a man at four hundred paces, and they had learned to be quite cool under fire.

Men like Johan and the brutal experience of battle had forged the regiment into as tough a regiment as he could recall ever seeing. These men made up but one regiment of many. The Iowa and other western regiments he had seen were every bit as tough as his own, and a whole lot more so than most of the regiments he had dealt with in the old country. He would pit most any regiment he had seen in this army against any Redcoat or French one. Those old country regiments might look prettier, but when it came time to march or to fight, Johan wanted these men beside him.

They had all heard the rumors that Atlanta had been wrecked, and every man in the regiment knew Hood had spent the last month running all through north Georgia with Sherman chasing the bastard. Hood had learned, though; open battles with this army led to disasters on par with Peachtree Creek, Atlanta and Ezra Church, which were not the kind of outcomes Hood wanted. And if Hood attacked a fortified post, he faced consequences the like of Allatoona.

"Sergeant, where we headed? Any guesses?" Seth asked from behind him.

"My money is on Savannah or Charleston. Vicksburg split them once and so either of those cities would split them again, and prove to everybody they are whipped," Johan said as he stepped around a deep rut in the road.

"What about Mobile?" A couple of other men agreed with Seth's question.

"It started in Charleston. And Savannah is another big port city with both in striking distance of the other. It will be one, with the other being the next."

Johan turned and looked down the column; he could just see Mina's cart with the regimental ambulance. He grinned at the thought of her driving the regimental ammunition and ration cart. The cart was full to capacity with her tent, pots and pans, two barrels of salt pork, four boxes of hard tack and three thousand rounds of ammunition. He could just see Mina; she looked tired, the reins gripped loosely in her hands. She was wearing a cast off cavalry jacket and an almost new army dress hat.

A staff ass rode along the column, well mounted on a powerful bay. He reined in hard beside the regimental officers. Johan could not hear the orders but he could guess them. More skirmishers on the flanks. Wheeler was out there somewhere, gobbling up stragglers and murdering them. They all knew the stories and had heard the rumors. Some had seen the bodies and their dire promises. Johan grinned coldly; two could play at that game, and the time for a reckoning would come.

"Lieutenant Boraas, take Sergeant Steele and first platoon two hundred yards to the right as skirmishers." The war and Allatoona in particular had taken a lot out of the Captain. He looked haggard and tired to the bone. The promotion of Jacob Boraas to Lieutenant had been a superb idea, one endorsed by every man in the company.

William might have liked that rank, but he would have to make do as a new corporal instead.

Jacob motioned to Johan; the first platoon peeled off of the column and deployed as skirmishers. There was no need for spoken commands. The men knew their business and knew it well. Good Lord, but Johan was proud. He had trained most of these men and he had little doubt that they were every bit as tough as the men he had campaigned with across North Africa and the Crimea. Yet most still maintained their humanity; the war had not turned them into murderers. If anything, the opposite was true. They had been repeatedly harassed by guerrillas and had never once lashed out at civilians. Oh, they had burned property, true, but never once had they murdered a civilian in retaliation no matter how much some had deserved it.

Johan watched Emmanuel moving with Little Foot. The death of Nate had changed Emmanuel. No longer was there any kindness in his eyes; cold hatred had turned Emmanuel into one of the Captain's killers, a man every bit as hard as Johan. It was a continuing concern, for Emmanuel and his wounded mind would be all too likely to get himself and maybe others killed in his pursuit of vengeance. But Little Foot worked well with him, and they seemed to enjoy the silence of each other's company.

Johan had assigned Bryce to the new recruits and the entire mess had worked to bring the new men up to scratch.

They were so young, eager and willing to learn. Andrew Henderson, Brian Trevor and Duncan German. Andrew was a bit of a prankster with aspirations toward the officer ranks, and that might get him into trouble with some of the veterans. Brian insisted on keeping his hair far too long which made him the target of many a joke. Duncan was a solid young man, in earnest to prove himself a soldier... perhaps he too eager. Johan thought all three would make

233

good soldiers, if the war allowed them to survive long enough.

He missed Josh, but he would be a long while in hospital. At that, he was luckier than Sebastian or Nate. At least Josh had a hope for the future. He should have made Bryce stay too, but the man had walked out of the hospital to answer morning roll with the regiment.

They moved through the pine trees, quick and careful. There were no recent signs of Wheeler's cavalry, though that did not mean they were not nearby. Pushing through the trees, they kept the column just in sight of the reserve.

"Sergeant!" Emmanuel's voice shattered the stillness. Johan could just make out the man waving to him. Johan motioned to Bryce to bring the new men and he started out at a jog towards Emmanuel. He stopped short as he neared Emmanuel. Little Foot had disappeared into the trees, leaving the carnage to Emmanuel and Johan's small party.

Before him in a small clearing was a sight unlike anything even he had ever seen. A score of bodies lay strewn across the ground. From their dress they had not been soldiers but runaway slaves. There were the bodies of men, women and children; wild hogs had been at some of them. The elements had bloated and twisted them so that they barely looked like people anymore. There were the ruins of a dry camp nearby; bits of canvas tarp that had been used for a tent, cook pots and a spilled fire.

It did not take a soldier to know what had happened here. Home Guard or some of Wheeler's men had found these runaways and made them pay with their lives for daring to seek freedom. From the condition of the bodies this had happened days before. That likely made Wheeler's men innocent of these sins, and the guilty party the local Home Guard or a slave patrol.

Johan looked at the corpses in disgust and wished the foulest death he could imagine upon those who would murder women and children... though he rather suspected they would be viewed as heroes by some. There was no time to bury these people, and he doubted many in the army would be willing to be detailed as a burial party for dead slaves.

"My God, one's alive!" Emmanuel let out a shout and Johan ran to him.

It was true. A woman lay in a small depression, looking up at them with fevered eyes. Both of her legs had been broken and the rotten smell that came off of her told them that she should have been dead.

Emmanuel knelt and offered his canteen to the woman's lips; she drank greedily then coughed weakly.

"Youalls Yankees?" Her voice was strained with the effort and her dark face contorted in pain as she spoke.

"Yes, from Minnesota." Emmanuel said as a tear leaked from his eye.

"Take my baby. Please, I promised her to see freedom." The woman shook in pain as she spoke and moved a pine straw covered log aside, revealing an infant sheltered within.

Johan looked at Emmanuel and then down at the woman.

Emmanuel answered for him by slinging his rifle across his back as he knelt down beside the dying woman. "I will see her to freedom; you got my word." Emmanuel's voice brooked no argument from Johan.

The woman grasped Emmanuel's hand and squeezed. "You promise... you promised. You keep your promise, you hear?" Her voice strained with the effort. She had clearly forced herself to live until her child was safe, and now she could let go. Johan hung his head, as did the other men, though whether in prayer or shame for what had been done Johan did not know.

The woman watched Emmanuel pick up her daughter and began to sing. The words were foreign to every man standing in that clearing, haunting and beautiful. The men stood there listening in silence. The baby began to cry. They were small whimpers at first, then grew in volume until they drowned out the dying woman's song. How she had the strength to sing was a marvel.

Emmanuel cradled the baby in his arms rocking her back and forth and patting her back as he did so. The baby quieted down and silence fell across the clearing like a blanket.

"What's her name?" Andrew asked, not taking his eyes off of the body of the child's mother.

"Freedom. Her name is Freedom," Emmanuel said as he cooed to the baby.

"Emmanuel, take Freedom back to Mina. She can care for it for now," Johan said.

Emmanuel snapped his head up and looked hard at Johan. "Her! She's a girl, not an 'it.'" He turned on his heel and started back toward the column.

Johan stared at Emmanuel's retreating back a moment. Was this a sign of a return to sanity? He turned to the new men. "Andrew, make a marker. 'Freedom's Mother.' The rest of you cover her up as best you can. Bryce, get Seth and have him say some words over her. Twenty minutes."

Johan turned towards the rest of the reserve and Lieutenant Boraas; Jacob needed to know there was a new recruit in the company.

Seth looked down at the body of the woman in the shallow hole Bryce and Brian had deepened into a grave. One of the men had wrapped her in his blanket, and the US was carefully set over her chest. The marker Andrew had crafted was simple but poignant; he had used his bayonet to scratch the words 'Freedom's Mother' into a simple cross of cut limbs, then used a brand to burn the words into the cross. It was fixed now over her head, tied to the tree that would be her marker. She was on her way to a better place than this. No whip would again touch her back, or shackles bind her legs. Andrew knelt down and put a pair of coins over her eyes and pulled the blanket over her face.

Seth lowered his head and closed his eyes. "Good Lord, we place this woman into the ground and pray that her soul finds the gates to heaven with no trouble. In Ephesians it is said You decided to choose us long ago in keeping with Your plan. You work out everything to fit Your plan and purpose. We pray, Lord, that this gentle mother was able to fulfill Your plan before she was so cruelly ripped from this world.

"Lord God, You said in Luke that Jesus was sent to proclaim the release to the captives. Jesus; we beg of you to lead this woman to her rightful place with you in heaven.

"Amen."

Seth looked up to see every man with his head bowed and fifty paces on he could see Sergeant Steele cross himself in the way of the Catholics.

Seth looked about the clearing. The men had gathered the remains of the other dead into a pile in the center of the clearing. No one knew their names. They were but a few more of the nameless masses sacrificed in the cause of slavery and treason. He watched the men move out in skirmish order. The war would not wait even long enough to bury the innocent dead. People murdered, simply because of the color of their skin. Seth wondered how such things fit into God's plan for this country. There had been enough blood spilled to stain the country red. Could it ever be enough to wash away the stain of slavery?

Seth looked back at the clearing. Those people would be forgotten, no gravestone marked their place and he knew the local white population likely neither knew nor cared for their fate. Their murders meant nothing to anyone but the men who found them. Seth knew he should never wish ill upon anyone – it was not a Christian sentiment – but he felt himself pray nonetheless. "Lord, please visit justice upon those who would do such a thing; show them the same mercy they showed those in that clearing."

Mina looked down at the baby she held in her arms. Emmanuel had handed her the baby and she had melted. So pretty a girl child. Freedom was a perfect name. Little Foot brought her a dipper of milk from an officer's mare. Other laundresses brought scraps of clothes for diapers and bedding. And Johan, bless his soul, had given her a bottle of his fine Scotch to use in cleaning the child.

Mina ran her hand through the child's wisp of hair and caressed her face cooing to her as she did so. She stopped as the baby began to whimper. She started to sing, a lullaby she remembered from her childhood. As she finished, she looked up from the sleeping baby. Perhaps a score of men stood there looking at her, some with their hats off and held in their hands. A look of peace graced their faces, and more than a few eyes were no longer dry.

She grinned as Jacob Boraas stepped forward. "Mrs. Mina, might I hold the child a few minutes? I haven't seen my own little one in most of a year, and I'd like to just hold her."

Mina looked at him suspiciously. "Have you washed your hands?"

He meekly held out his hands for her to inspect and Mina handed Freedom to the big man. She watched him gently rock the baby in his arms. Other men from the company stood close around, Kevin tickled Freedom's nose with a chicken feather and smiled as she laughed in her sleep. What a child could do to such men as this. They were hard as steel, toughed in the fires of war; but they melted at the sight of such a precious child. There was hope for these men with such a tiny angel in their midst.

Johan often spoke of the beautiful Angel of Death; little Miss Freedom was an angel all of her own. She was an angel of innocence of the kind most of these men had almost forgotten existed.

She looked past the group. There was Emmanuel sitting on the ground whittling on a stick; he had said he would make her a rattle. Johan was smoking his pipe as he leaned against a tree beside Emmanuel and talked to Seth as they watched the little gathering around the baby.

If anyone hurt this baby these men would kill that person, of that she had no doubt. And if the good Lord decided to take her, it would shatter them. Such a thing would turn their hearts cold, and God help those they deemed responsible.

Mina was surprised that Seth was not there looking over her shoulder, praying for the baby. She knew Seth was bothered by the war; by what he had seen and done. He had a good soul, one torn asunder by the hatred this war had created. Though she reminded herself not to, Mina still couldn't help but think of him as the boy she had first known from that winter in Minnesota. His entry to manhood had been brutal, as the war forced his growth. Mina doubted Seth's mother or beloved little sister could ever understand the changes that had scarred him. The war had done the same to all it touched, soldier and civilian alike.

The army was moving quickly; a dozen or more miles a day with brigades taking turns tearing up the rails. Wheeler could do nothing but harass and while he wasn't really doing that very well, any straggler was taking his life into his hands. Wheeler's men would offer him no mercy, and if he was lucky a bullet would end it. If not, they would join the ranks of Wheeler's tortured dead.

They were on skirmish duty every three days or so. That was good, as it kept the veterans on their toes, and taught the new men what they needed to know.

Johan puffed on his pipe while he watched men from B Company load a wagon with forage and dreamt of that fine bottle of cognac he had liberated from that last plantation house. They were doing an excellent job. There were farmers among those men who knew their trade. They already had another wagon loaded with feed corn for the cavalry and artillery, and would leave just enough hay to get the barn burning. Twelve cattle, a half dozen horses and a half hundred pigs were headed back to the column from this plantation. The house was already burning, and every chicken and another two or three score pigs had been gathered by the slaves fleeing this place.

"Sergeant!" Andrew yelled at him. He looked a little out of breath. "Corporal Young sent me at the double quick to fetch you and the Lieutenant."

"Where... Why? Speak up." Johan asked around his pipe.

"Trouble at the next farm," he puffed, still out of breath. "Maybe a mile up the road."

"Wheeler?" Johan demanded feeling his stomach clench.

"No, worse. You'll see."

"Go get the Lieutenant and bring him. He is at the well soaking his feet. I'll take the rest of the mess on the double quick." Johan turned to Seth. "Let's go; double quick."

The two men took off, their weapons instinctively raised to right shoulder shift. It was more scrub pine forest with more of a deeply rutted path cutting through it than any kind of real road. They covered the mile in well under ten minutes.

Andrew calling it a farm had been generous; a clapboard shack and chicken shed with the roof falling in were the only buildings. The lack of livestock showed the place had already been stripped clean by foragers.

Bryce moved towards them, face red and eyes wide with rage. Kevin had tied a length of thick rope into a noose and was working on another with a cold look of fury upon his face as he stared off into the distance. Emmanuel, Little Foot and the new men were nowhere to be seen.

"What happened?" Johan demanded.

Bryce said nothing, only motioned Johan to the house. "Little Foot and Emmanuel are up the road keeping watch, Will is in a tree keeping watch to the south. Go look in the house," he hissed. "We'll be hanging some men."

241

Johan looked askance at Seth, who shrugged, and the two headed up the stairs into the house. His eyes took a moment to adjust to the darkness as he strode through the open door.

A pair of Springfields with two sets of leathers piled on top and a new Henry rifle laid beside them. Three men, two wearing the uniform of Union soldiers, knelt on the floor with their hands clasping their ankles behind their backs; the third man was naked but for an undershirt and someone had beaten him thoroughly. One eye was swollen shut and his nose and probably cheekbone had been broken. The way his right hand looked it had been broken as well. Ropes bound none of their hands, for Brian and Duncan had bayonets fixed on loaded weapons. Johan recognized none of the men kneeling on the floor.

"What the hell?" Johan demanded. Then he saw the woman.

'Girl' would have been more appropriate. She was all of thirteen, a pretty child with long blond hair that had been dragged through the dirt a time or two recently. She was clothed in Brian's blanket. An angry welt colored her right cheekbone. And tears had cut sharp paths through the dirt and grime that covered her pretty face.

Brian handed Johan a sack coat with Lieutenant's boards on the shoulders. Johan felt the blood rise up in his face, and Brian stepped back nervously.

"Seth, give the girl their blankets and the contents of their pockets," Johan said coldly as he fixed his bayonet.

"The Lieutenant has a hundred dollars in gold coin…"

Duncan stopped as Johan looked at him. "Had,"Johan corrected with a snarl. "Give it to the girl. Then go tell Kevin he will only need two ropes."

"Sergeant, listen to me. That's a hundred dollars in good gold coin to keep your mouth shut. She's just a Rebel whore..." The officer's mouth snapped shut as Johan turned on him.

"Stand up," Johan ordered. The three men did as they were ordered and Seth quickly pulled a pocket knife, watch and two dollars from the pockets of the privates. Johan motioned to the two enlisted men. "You two outside."

They complied and went out the door with Duncan close behind. The two privates were young, their uniforms fairly new. New recruits, most likely.

They would not live to be veterans.

Seth knelt beside the girl and prayed as she wept. Brian looked on.

The Lieutenant swallowed. "Sergeant, no one has to know about this. No one wants a court martial..."

Bryce smashed the officer in the balls with the butt of his rifle then hit him in the face when he started to curl up in pain. The man screamed in agony from the crushed testicle and shattered nose. Johan looked on in approval.

"Brian, take those weapons out of here," Johan said as he looked at the girl. "Make sure Boraas gets that Henry." She was about the age of William's little sister. "Is this your home, girl?"

She looked at him with eyes so filled with tears of hate they fairly glowed. "No."

"Seth, get her out of here," Johan growled. Seth looked at him then reached down and took the girl by the arm.

The girl screamed her fear and fought Seth, pummeling his chest with small fists. He caught her fists and spoke quietly.

Whatever he said penetrated her fury, and she stopped fighting him. He spoke further to her and she followed him. Only Seth could reason with or even touch a child so badly mistreated.

When the two left the house Johan motioned Bryce to the officer and he began beating him. A half dozen good solid hits with the butt of a rifle and Johan felt better. A small measure of revenge for the girl had been attained. The son of a bitch was a bloody mess. It was time he met an angel... though that meeting might take a while.

"Get up," Johan ordered.

The officer cried out in pain but did as he was ordered. He took hold of the door frame to keep from falling. Johan planted his boot in the middle of the Lieutenant's back and pushed. The officer sprawled onto the ground at the base of the steps with a groan. Johan reached down and took hold of the man's hair and forced his head up towards the two condemned men.

"Watch them die, you cowardly son of a bitch," he hissed. The two privates were standing beneath a thick tree limb with nooses around their necks and ropes looped up and over the limb.

Kevin and William were on one rope and Bryce and Duncan on the other.

Johan took one look. "Run them up." The four men pulled on the ropes yanking the condemned men a few feet off of the ground. They kicked and fought, using their hands to desperately try to hold onto the rope and keep from strangling. Johan's men tied the ropes around the trunk of another tree. It took minutes for them to die and all present watched in grim silence.

"Leave them." Bryce said. Johan nodded his head in approval.

"Stand," Johan ordered.

"Please, I don"t want to die!" the officer begged as he obeyed.

Johan stabbed him in the belly with his bayonet, twisted his rifle and then slapped the stock to disembowel the officer.

The scream of agony cut across the farmstead like a knife. Johan knelt beside the officer and cleaned his bayonet on man's shirt as he moaned and cried from the pain.

Then Johan stood and spit on the him.

When he turned, he saw Seth and Brian both looking at him in horror with the girl between them. Her expression was a cold smile.

"Give him nothing; Seth, you will not pray over him."

Seth started to say something, then evidently thought better of it.

Boraas and Andrew chose that moment to come jogging up. "Steele, what the hell have you done?" demanded the Lieutenant.

There was no chance to answer him, as Emmanuel and Little Foot came running into the clearing. "Reb cavalry!" Emmanuel shouted.

Boraas swore viciously and turned to the men. "Get under cover!"

Johan walked over and retrieved the dead Lieutenant's drawers. He quickly tied them to a long branch. "Steele what in the hell are you doing?" Jacob demanded.

Johan handed Kevin his rifle and cartridge box. "Will can tell you what happened here, if I do not come back." He walked to the girl. She was wearing the dead Lieutenant's jacket over her torn clothing, and a blanket was draped around her shoulders. "Come, I will take you to your people." He took her the arm, the girl moving willingly, and they began walking in the direction Emmanuel and Little Foot had come from.

Johan took a deep breath as they walked towards the cavalry that he knew had to be just out of sight. He had no doubt they knew where his men were, and probably had an idea of their numbers. Wheeler's men were all veterans and in no way foolish enough to charge prepared infantry.

He did not think of Mina. If he had, he probably never would have started this walk. It took only a few minutes to reach where he could see the enemy. His stomach clenched as he saw them; probably thirty cavalry. Texans, the stars on hats and the way they sat their horses made that obvious to him. Half a dozen pistols pointed his direction and he could hear the murmur as they saw the girl beside him.

He raised his improvised flag of truce high.

"What you want, Yank? Gonna surrender?" The man who spoke wore no sword and sat with one leg thrown over the pommel of his saddle.

Johan saw no officer in the group, only this one sergeant, a corporal and two dozen privates. The Sergeant's horse was a powerful gray gelding that looked well cared, for as did the Colt pistol that lay naked in his hand. The stripes on his jacket had faded to an almost white color, his clothing was ragged with the wear and tear that comes from an old uniform. A fighting man of long duration.

"This girl is one of yours," Johan said. "She was hurt, and needs to be taken to safety."

The Texas Sergeant looked appraisingly at Johan. "You bastards dishonor her? Bringing her to us ain't gonna keep us from hangin' you." He spat a stream of tobacco juice onto the ground in front of Johan.

246

"We already dealt with the bastards who were respon-sible," Johan said, releasing the girl's arm to fill his pipe.

"Sure you did, Yank, sure you did." The man's voice fairly dripped with scorn.

"Hanged two and the other you may have if you like," Johan said with that old grin. "But you will have to wait for my men to leave."

One of the Texans laughed. He was a blond youngster with eyes as blue as the sky. "We can take you any time we want."

Johan nodded his head in agreement. "Yes, you could, and there would be the plus of the extra horses."

The Sergeant looked hard at Johan. "What extra horses?"

"The dozen or so with empty saddles you will be leading away from the fight." He kept his smile steady, his eyes on the Sergeant. "I have three of the finest shooters you could imagine, and the rest of the men are quite good as well. They will not go quietly or easily." Johan shook his head and looked at the girl, then demanded, "I came to get this girl help. Can you care for her or not?"

The Sergeant looked from Johan to the girl. "Leave her. We'll see her to safety. Do you ever play poker, Yank?"

"No. I only wager on sure things." Johan said.

"Go on, then. Get your men out of here. You run a good bluff, Yank."

"Take care of her." Johan said as he lit his pipe. He looked from the girl to the Sergeant and spoke around the pipe stem. "When a man bluffs, sometimes he had best have the cards to make it stick." He turned and walked away relishing the pipe; never had tobacco tasted so good.

Johan could hear the blue eyed blond boy ask, "What the hell did he mean by that?"

"He meant we would have lost half a dozen men hitting those bastards down the road. Men like that... they're the reason we lost." The Sergeant had a naturally commanding voice and it carried.

"We ain't beat, we got God on our side," the blond boy said passionately.

The Texan sergeant laughed. "I've seen more than my share of the devil, but damned little of god. We lost when they started east out of Atlanta. We can't stop 'em and there sure as hell ain't nobody else stepping up to do the job."

"They're the spawn of the devil," the blond boy snarled.

"No. Wish they were. They're men... men of flesh and blood. That we couldn't stop them merely shows their iron conviction."

Johan appreciated the comment said to his back. It came from a fighting man, and because of that it meant more than any mention in dispatches ever would. The respect of a foe was what a soldier appreciated. Not the eagerness for the killing or contempt for death, for when one grows contemptuous of death the Angel of Death notices you. Johan had spent his life learning that.

As Johan walked into the clearing, he saw Lieutenant Boraas standing in the doorway of the shack with his new Henry in hand. No one else was in sight. At least one man would be on the roof, with the others sheltered behind cover. That dozen saddles would have been emptied in a hurry had those Texans come rushing in. Men like Emmanuel, Kevin and William had learned to shoot to kill. But those that fell before their weapons had been soldiers, men... men of flesh, blood and iron conviction.

The war was over. There would be another big battle or two, but the *war* was over. The Rebels could not stop them and all knew it; only the fanatics and fools would remain and they could be hunted down and dealt with. The Rebellion was well and truly finished, and when they reached and took Savannah it would be an evident truth to all.

The war had been won by the likes of the men in his mess. Citizen soldiers, not professional button polishers nor even old campaigners like himself.

"Hell to pay, Steele!" Boraas said angrily. "Damned sure should have waited for me."

Johan shrugged. "You might have thought they deserved a court martial and a trial. They received a soldier's justice."

Jacob looked down at the fine Henry rifle in his hands. "I suppose you're right. Damn Wheeler's men for hanging them. Saved us the trouble, I suppose."

Johan chuckled. Fine officer, that Lieutenant Boraas.

1883

Those of us who lived through the War can never forget. We cannot imagine life without it; we think of things as happening before, during or after the War. The War was the defining moment of our lives; when we found our mettle. I lost good friends, men who I had come to regard as brothers. Sometimes, I visit the stones of friends who have died since the War and I wonder what their lives would have been like if there had been no War; would they have been better men, or worse?

I recently buried a good friend, a man who I came to look upon as the older brother I never had. I have lived my life through his daughter and through the two girls of my little sister. I have never married; I'm not certain I have every truly loved a woman. While I have appreciated the beauty or spirit of some women, I have never really met the woman I wished to live my life with. I think I should blame that upon the War, as it changed me, and in many ways killed my spirit. The things I saw and some of the things I did stained and scarred my soul. We all saw and did things we will never be able to forget, and perhaps never forgive ourselves for.

I am proud to say that I did nothing that shamed me and was shamed by only one of my friends... and that may well have been the shame of a naïve child. I am proud of my service and of my comrades as we served a cause greater than ourselves. We saved our nation. Before the War I was a boy, a child with dreams. The War changed me, as it changed all that it touched.

My closest friend was Johan Steele. He called me his "Copain." I learned that in French it means friend. He had been a soldier in the French Army fighting in the Crimea and in North Africa. In the years before the War he came to Minnesota via Charleston and Vicksburg, traveling north on the Mississippi, and made a sparse living trading with the Sioux. I think in a way he preferred the red man to the white.

His wife, Mrs. Mina, was an angel; I think in a way I came to love her. She saved many a life with her herbs and poultices, but I think it is our very souls that we owe her. She gave us hope and a glimpse at humanity at times when all else had been lost. She followed her husband all the way to the Sea and beyond.

Before the War I dreamed of being a harness maker, blacksmith, teacher and many other noble professions. But I made a good soldier for four long years, and after that I have lived the life of a humble farmer. There were ten of us in the mess at the beginning; four died as a result of wounds and two more would go home carrying the awful physical scars of War. More than fifty more would fall in battle and countless died in hospital either from wounds incurred on the battlefield or to the scourge of disease. I remember many of their faces well; it is a class of memory that has haunted my soul since.

Once, after the War and my return home my sister asked

me if I felt regret for killing. I believe the answer I gave was a mirror to what Johan said before our first battle when I was seized by the fear and loathing for the blood that was soon to be shed. His words were poignant and I remember them well. "When a man sets out to kill you, it becomes a simple thing to kill him. It is kill or be killed. Killing is not an easy thing, nor should it be. That first realization that you have just ended a man's hopes and dreams, and all that he was is no more, should haunt you. But that next death will be easier and trouble you less. After a while the death and suffering numbs you and the suffering of others no longer affects you; it is then that killing becomes the trade of a soldier." I do not believe she ever looked at me in the same way again.

I returned from the War a changed man, as did any who

the War touched. My sister lost friends and neighbors who went to War and failed to return. She suffered through the years of want that the War created. Thank God the War never touched her directly. She never saw our fences torn down to feed the voracious cook fires of the army, or our livestock taken to feed an army's stomach, and the homestead was never converted to a hospital. Thank the Lord she was never made a refugee by the ill fortunes of a retreating army.

I have gathered all of the letters that my sister kept, nearly one hundred; I have also kept correspondence from a young laundress that graced our camp, and two score letters I wrote to Maxine, a young woman who became my friend when I needed one most. Much of her own story was told in those letters to me. Now, most of twenty years later, I read these letters and reflect upon that terrible time. Memories fade and it is intriguing to me what I remember most vividly. The suffering and deaths of others are far too vivid and will not fade. The smell of Mrs. Mina's fresh bread and beans cooking in the fire are still sharp. I do not know why I have kept these letters for so long. No one but the various authors is likely to remember them.

Of the surviving members of my mess, William was killed in an accident helping to build the Trans-Continental Railroad. Emmanuel and Joshua disappeared into the vast west like so many others, never to be seen or heard from again. Bryce went back to the life of a sailor upon the great lakes for a time, and took up the quiet life of a lighthouse keeper in '79. Only Kevin and I remain near to where we grew up. I raise horses and have made a good life of it. Kevin is a successful gunsmith and active in the GAR, a well thought of man in the community. Johan and Mina made a successful go of it as tavern keepers.

Johan passed last year in an alcohol-induced coma, his memories finally overtaking him. He willed me his copy of Blackstone with a letter I had never seen, written by my mother, tucked into its pages. He is survived by a beautiful daughter, Freedom, and his angel of a wife that he loved more than life itself.

Mrs. Mina and I eventually taught him his letters and he did quite well by our teaching. I greatly miss his letters to me. Our young friend Sven, originally named Seven, has grown to be a good and true man of God. He is the successful preacher of a small church in St Paul. He has come far from the half-drowned rat who presented himself to us during the Vicksburg campaign. I look to him with great pride and appreciation that I helped to turn him from a desperate and ignorant child into a good man of God. In Sven we accomplished something noble and good.

In the end, though, I wonder if we did not win the War only to lose the peace; we freed four million people from bondage, only to see them held down by those we freed them from. I have been told that things have not changed in the southland. Those who held sway before the War hold sway still. Those who were poor before the War remain so, with little hope of improvement in their lives.

I hope the words compiled in this book have helped to explain the men and women who tried to bring hope, freedom and a better future to this nation. But the generations of our children must continue to shape that future. I hope and pray that you shall appreciate my efforts and perhaps garner a greater understanding of the actions of the men who saved this imperfect Union.

God Bless and Keep You, Dear Reader;

Seth Barnaby

"And to think, this was all started by an obituary."

Shane Christen is a professional amateur Living Historian who revels in dressing up in funny clothes and sleeping on the ground under the stars. His passion is history, particularly 19th century US history. He is the father to three of his own children and a couple more that aren't his but who occasionally will call him Dad or Uncle.

An electronic security technician by trade, Shane has a thing for American Civil War firearms, levels and Archimedes drills and axes and adzes and God only knows what next. He is a consummate carny barker who could probably sell ice to an Eskimo if he ever used his powers for evil.

His wife, Bobbie, is his angel and he is fond of reminding her of that, lest he wake up dead some morning.

www.ingramcontent.com/pod-product-compliance
Lightning Source LLC
Chambersburg PA
CBHW020554180626
46810CB00007B/2504